"What is it you *want*?"

His smile wolfish, Keir replied, "You know quite well what I want, Sera."

"Revenge, presumably."

"Revenge, certainly. But there's something I want a great deal more. You in my bed," Keir told her.

"There are plenty of other women," Sera insisted.

"It happens to be *you* I want."

"I've already told you I'm not for sale to any man."

"Then if money won't do the trick, I'll have to think of some other way to get you...."

Lee Wilkinson

THE DETERMINED HUSBAND

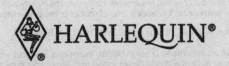

HARLEQUIN®

TORONTO • NEW YORK • LONDON
AMSTERDAM • PARIS • SYDNEY • HAMBURG
STOCKHOLM • ATHENS • TOKYO • MILAN • MADRID
PRAGUE • WARSAW • BUDAPEST • AUCKLAND

ISBN 0-373-12183-0

THE DETERMINED HUSBAND

First North American Publication 2001.

CHAPTER ONE

THE elevator descended smoothly and sighed to a halt. As the doors slid open, like a prisoner scenting freedom Sera stepped out and, her rubber-soled trainers squeaking a little on the marble floor, hurried across the Warburton Building's impressive, chandelier-hung foyer.

At this very early hour it was deserted, but as she approached the smoked-glass doors, the blue-uniformed night-security guard appeared.

His seamed face breaking into a welcoming beam, he said, 'Morning, Miss Reynolds,' and decided, with fatherly concern, that she was still looking a mite thin and pale.

'Morning, Bill. How's your lumbago?'

'Not as bad as it might be.'

He surveyed her navy and white track suit, her shiny nose, and the long, silky black hair caught up in a ponytail. She looked no older than fifteen in that get-up, though he knew from a previous conversation that she was twenty four, the same age as his own Nancy.

'Off for your usual run round the Park?' he asked.

Sera, who was by no means an athlete, only walked or jogged gently according to her mood, but she answered pleasantly, 'That's right.'

'Well, you've sure got a nice day for it.'

Bill was a creature of habit, and the same conversation took place each morning, the only difference being his last comment, which changed according to the weather.

He held open the side door for her, and she thanked him with a smile. She was a pretty little thing, he thought for the umpteenth time, and, unlike a lot of the tenants, she always managed a pleasant word and a cheerful smile, in spite of an ever-present air of sadness.

Outside it was cool and fresh, the sky a pale, innocent blue. Fifth Avenue lay as quiet as a sleeping babe in the after-dawn lull, undisturbed as yet by the bustle of the day.

In Central Park the green leafy trees looked newly washed, the flowers heavy with dew. Swirls of early morning mist hung over the grass like translucent ghosts lingering on after some spooky midnight gathering.

Taking her usual route, Sera began to walk at a good pace, enjoying the coolness of the air with its promise of a scorching day to come.

Other than a solitary jogger in the distance, she seemed to have the Park to herself. She liked the sensation of being alone. This was the only hour of the day when, free from the stifling atmosphere of Martin's luxurious apartment, she felt truly at ease, unpressured, able to be herself.

That, apart from the much-needed exercise, was the reason she treasured these early morning outings. It was also the reason she kept them a secret from Martin.

Kathleen, his attractive, black-haired Irish nurse knew, but was sympathetic and said nothing.

Sera was truly grateful.

If Martin found out, she knew instinctively that he would find some way to put a stop to them. With a jealous possessiveness that amounted almost to paranoia, he wanted her by his side every minute of every hour of every day.

Though having the utmost sympathy with his bitterness and frustration at being in pain and confined to a wheelchair, and suffering for him vicariously, Sera was frayed.

She could only feel guiltily thankful when Kathleen occasionally relieved her of the burden by insisting that, after a morning of business, he should rest alone in his room for a couple of hours.

When that happened, still wanting her within call, he would turn to Sera and order peremptorily, 'Don't go out.'

'No, I won't,' she'd assure him.

After the stick would come the carrot. 'When I've had my afternoon therapy, we'll take a drive.'

But she was weary of the specially adapted, air-conditioned limousine, of sitting when she would sooner have been walking, of having Martin beside her when she would rather have been alone...

Miserable and ashamed of herself, she broke off the disloyal thought. No doubt things would be a great deal easier when he was able fully to resume his business life.

Martin was a vigorous go-getter and found any kind of inactivity or restriction irksome, to say the least. His temper ready to flare at any moment, he had made a difficult, demanding patient, and even Kathleen's imperturbable good humour had sometimes been stretched to the limit.

It had been a great fillip to him when, only a few days ago, his doctors had given him a positive progress report.

Though he might never be able to run a marathon or jump hurdles, and he would be left with a slight limp, in a matter of months he should be relatively free from pain and on his feet once more.

Normally a very sociable man, since the accident he'd hardly seen a soul, apart from his sister, Cheryl, and his brother-in-law, Roberto.

Hating the idea of people seeing him in what he termed 'This damned contraption', he wouldn't go out—his only excursions had been afternoon drives in the car—and he'd refused to invite anyone to the apartment.

His thirty-third birthday, which fell on the following Saturday, would have gone unmarked. But bolstered by

the good news, and encouraged by Cheryl, whose suggestion it was, he'd started to make plans for a weekend party
at Pine Cove, his house in the Hamptons.

'How many people were you thinking of inviting?'
Cheryl had asked.

'Perhaps twenty or so to stay at the house—though we'll
need to warn Mrs Simpson—and some of the neighbours
for the Saturday evening...'

'Right. Roberto and I are having a break at Fiddler's
Cottage, so you can leave all the arrangements to me. I'll
talk to Mrs Simpson, phone or fax the invitations, and
arrange for the caterers. We'll need plenty of champagne.
I think news like this calls for a celebration!'

As for Sera, the doctors' verdict had been like some
precious gift. She had been secretly terrified that Martin
might never walk again, and her relief was so great that
she had broken down and wept for joy.

The rather less than joyous reaction that had followed
later had been a purely personal one. With the promise of
an almost complete recovery, their wedding day had suddenly loomed so much closer.

Martin was already talking about early October as a possibility, and she felt as though a silken noose was tight-
ening around her neck.

Sometimes, when she had temporarily escaped like this,
Sera toyed with the idea of never going back.

But, of course, it wasn't really an option.

Apart from her board and lodging, her job as Martin's
PA was an unpaid one. As though afraid she would leave
him if she were independent, he never gave her any cash.

When, one day, she had pointed out quietly that there
were certain small things she needed to buy, he'd said,
'Buy anything you want, and charge it,' which had effec-

tively prevented her from buying anything but absolute necessities.

The mere fact that she had nowhere to go, and no money, wouldn't have deterred her, but feeling morally bound to stay, she was as much a prisoner as if she'd been kept in chains...

The solitary jogger had long since disappeared and there wasn't a soul in sight as, still busy with her thoughts, she reached the stand of trees and the side track she usually took.

As she rounded the corner, as though he had been lying in wait for her, a man's tall dark figure suddenly appeared directly in her path. The sheer unexpectedness brought a startled cry to her lips.

'It's all right,' he reassured her quickly, 'there's no need to be scared.'

That voice, low-pitched and with a suggestion of huskiness, was one she would have recognized anywhere, a voice she would have left her grave for; that lean, darkly handsome face, was one she had loved and would love until the day she died.

Fright was replaced by shock so great that a wave of dizziness assailed her. Her brain robbed of blood and her legs of strength, she thought for a moment that she was going to faint.

Apparently he thought so too, because strong hands shot out and gripped her upper arms, steadying and supporting her.

'Keir!' He was the same, yet not the same. A little leaner perhaps, but the same virile physique was there, the same powerful structure of chest and shoulder.

His hard face was the same, the firm jaw, the strong nose and high cheekbones, the cleft chin, yet beside that chiselled mouth were lines of pain and disillusionment.

His impact was the same, the same intense sexuality that had once caused Sera to respond with such ardent abandonment, but now that sexuality was leashed, guarded.

Looking into those dark blue eyes with their thick sooty lashes, she whispered dazedly, 'What are you doing here?'

Indicating his black track suit and sweat band, he asked laconically, 'What does it look as if I'm doing?'

He'd jogged in the past, she knew. Was that what had subconsciously given her the idea for her early morning outings?

'B-but I thought you were living in England now,' she stammered.

'I decided it was high time I came back to see what was happening on the New York scene.' Then with no change of tone, 'So how is Rothwell?'

Wondering if he'd heard about the accident, she managed, 'Martin is doing well.'

'I heard Anglo American Finance made even bigger profits over this last year,' Keir remarked sardonically.

Reaching for her left hand, he studied the magnificent half-hoop of diamonds she wore. 'No wedding ring yet?'

'No.'

'Why not? Rothwell was mad about you.'

'He still is,' she replied flatly.

'Then, why the delay? You were all set to marry him last summer.' When she said nothing, he added caustically, 'He must be worth a tidy few millions by now, which should make you very happy.'

Stiffly, she said, 'I really don't know what you're getting at.'

'Oh, come on!'

'It doesn't matter to me how many millions he has.'

'There, now! And I thought it mattered very much.'

'Well, you were wrong.' Then helplessly she said, 'I can't understand what makes you think such a thing.'

'Forgive me if I point out that it didn't take you long to ditch me when someone with plenty of money came along.'

'I did nothing of the kind,' she denied angrily, and wondered how he could possibly blame *her* for the break-up. 'I've told you, I don't care about money.'

'Despite that assurance I can't help but believe things might have been different if I'd had any to spend on you.'

Gritting her teeth, she made to brush past him and walk on.

Keir turned and kept pace with her. 'I guess we just met at the wrong moment. When I moved into that apartment Downtown, falling in love was the last thing on my mind...'

No matter what he said now, she knew he had never loved her.

'I simply couldn't afford to fall in love. I had neither the time nor the money to spare. But fate plays funny tricks.'

Looking straight ahead, she kept walking.

Glancing at her pale, set face, he went on, 'I'd certainly never expected to bump into the woman of my dreams in a run-down apartment house...'

Sera's stride faltered as memories rushed in to swamp her...

Brand-new to the States, she had been living in a single room on the top floor of an old Brownstone in Lower Manhattan, when one warm evening in late spring they had bumped into one another.

Literally.

Head bent and deep in thought, she had been making

her way up the stairs, a brown paper carrier full of shopping clutched to her chest. At the same time a man had been coming down the next steep, uncarpeted flight of steps two at a time.

They reached the landing at the same instant, and a glancing blow from his shoulder made her drop her shopping and stagger back.

With great presence of mind he flung his arms around her to save her falling backwards, while various cartons and packages and a selection of fruit rolled and bounced gleefully down the steps.

Sera was five feet seven, but the man holding her was a good six feet and wide-shouldered. His beautiful, thickly lashed eyes were dark blue, his hair black, and with a tendency to curl.

He was dressed nicely, if casually, in stone-coloured jeans and an open-necked shirt. Lean-hipped, and carrying not an ounce of surplus weight, he looked like an athlete.

Tilting back her head, she focused on a tough, hard-boned face, with a cleft chin and a mouth that made butterflies dance in her stomach, and was suddenly breathless.

His dark eyes studied her flawless, heart-shaped face as he asked, 'Are you all right?' His voice was low-pitched and attractively husky.

Flustered, as much by his powerful sex appeal as by the narrowness of her escape, she answered a shade jerkily, 'Yes, thanks to you.'

His white smile set her pulses racing and she found herself unable to take her eyes off that chiselled mouth.

'Considering that I'm the one who almost knocked you flying in the first place, that's a nice, forgiving sort of way of looking at it.'

Tearing her gaze away, she told herself crossly that,

though she was a level-headed twenty-three-year-old, she was acting like some gauche schoolgirl.

Doing her best to sound casual, to hide the effect his nearness had on her, she managed lightly, 'I'm a nice, forgiving sort of person. And, to be honest, it was partly my fault.'

'Honest as well as forgiving,' he mocked gently. 'A woman in a million.' Before she could think of a suitable rejoinder, he added, 'And undeniably English.'

With unconscious pride, she told him, 'I'm half American…'

A level black brow was raised in surprise. 'I wouldn't have guessed.'

'Though I'd never been to the States until I got this chance to spend a year in the Wall Street branch of the company I work for.'

'Which is?'

'Anglo American Finance.'

'I know them,' he said at once. 'In fact, I've had business dealings with Martin Rothwell, the man who virtually owns Anglo American… What do you actually do?'

'I'm PA to Cheryl Rothwell, Mr Rothwell's sister. I met her when she came over to the London office and, after she discovered I was half American, she offered me this opportunity.'

'I see. So, which of your parents came from the States?'

'My mother. She was born in Boston.'

'Now, there's a coincidence! So was mine.'

'Oh… Then you *are* American? I couldn't be sure from your accent.'

'That's probably because, like yourself, I'm half American and half English. I was born and brought up in New York, but educated at Oxford.

'My paternal grandfather lives there, though our family originally came from Caithness.'

Just as he finished speaking, an orange, which had been balanced precariously on the edge of the top step, rolled off with a thump.

Glancing down, he said, 'Though it's much more fun standing here and holding you, I'd best rescue the shopping before it all ends up in the hall.'

As, bemused, she watched him deftly gather together the straying fruit and groceries, she knew that something special and momentous had happened to her.

Returning everything to the brown paper carrier, he remarked, 'Not a great deal of damage done, except to the eggs. They'll never be the same again.'

He looked ruefully at the damp, mangled package and added, 'I hope you weren't intending to have them for supper tonight?'

'I was as a matter of fact.'

His eyes on her left hand, which was bare of rings, he queried, 'Were you planning to eat alone?'

'Yes,' she admitted.

He clicked his tongue. 'On a Friday night, with the weekend just beginning?'

A shade defensively, she explained, 'I've only been in New York for a few days. I haven't had a chance to make friends.'

Though most people liked her, her natural shyness compounded by her upbringing, meant that she had never found it very easy to make friends.

He smote his forehead and cried theatrically, 'Poor little Annie! Alone and friendless in the big city!'

She was surprised into laughter by his clowning.

Gazing at her, fascinated, he exclaimed, 'Twin dimples as well as beautiful green eyes. My two favourite things.

Do you know, Annie, I've never met anyone with dimples *and* green eyes before.'

'My name's Sera,' she told him. 'Sera Reynolds.'

'And I'm Keir Sutherlands.'

They shook hands gravely.

'Well, Sera, after knocking you about and depriving you of your supper, the very least I can do is take you out for a pizza. What do you say?'

About to eagerly accept, she found herself recalling all the dire warnings her grandmother had dinned into her, and hesitated.

'If you don't like pizza we can have pasta instead.'

She half shook her head. 'I love pizza.'

Watching her face, he suggested evenly, 'But you've been warned about letting yourself be picked up by strange men?'

Her faint blush was answer enough.

He grinned. 'I may be a little odd in some ways but I hardly think I qualify as strange.'

Mischievously, she said, 'It might depend on one's definition of *strange*, and I'm afraid I don't know you well enough to judge.'

'We could easily remedy that.'

'Ah, but by then it might be too late.'

'A good point. In that case, let me reassure you as to my intentions, my status, and my propensities...

'I have no designs either on your purse or your person, I'm not married, or even mildly involved with anyone; and I've never been known to grow horns and a tail, or turn into a homicidal maniac, without warning.

'On the other hand, if you prefer a more positive approach, we're both Anglo-American, and I *do* live in the same building. Which means I count as a neighbour...'

'I'm not sure the latter is entirely reassuring,' she teased.

'I imagine even the Boston Strangler must have been somebody's neighbour.'

He pretended to be aggrieved. 'Of course, if you don't like the look of me, just say so. I may go and throw myself in the Hudson, but you've no need to feel any guilt...'

They were both enjoying the exchange, and she laughed. 'That's nice to know. I don't stand up too well to guilt.'

Studying her face, the clear, long-lashed almond eyes, the straight nose, the wide, generous mouth and softly rounded chin, he asked, 'How well do you stand up to a spot of friendly persuasion?'

'Not too well,' she admitted.

'Then, supposing I was to say it would make me very happy if you would come and share a pizza with me?'

'I can feel myself weakening.'

'Thank the Lord for that!' he exclaimed fervently. 'Now, suppose we go and dump the shopping before we both die of hunger? Which floor do you live on?'

'The top floor at the back. I have a bedsit.'

'Here, it's classed as one room apartment,' he told her with a grin, adding, as they turned to climb the stairs together. 'I live on the top at the front, so we really are neighbours.'

'It's a wonder we haven't met before,' she marvelled.

He shook his head. 'It's a wonder we've met now. You said you'd only lived here a few days. I haven't been here much longer myself. In this kind of building people can live next door to each other and never meet at all, unless they happen to keep the same hours.

'Normally I wouldn't be around at this time, but a client I was taking out to dinner called at the last minute to say he couldn't make it.

'Feeling at a loose end, I decided to come back and

change into something casual before grabbing a bite to eat.'

Smiling at her, he added, 'I'm very glad I did.'

The first few weeks of being in love—and she was madly, head-over-heels in love—had been the most wonderful weeks of her life.

She had discovered that Keir was everything she had ever wanted in a man, and more. As well as being exciting, and physically attractive, he proved to be good-tempered and intelligent, sensitive and compassionate, with a spiky sense of humour and a love of life that was infectious.

He was also a workaholic: at his Wall Street office most evenings until gone nine, and a good part of every weekend.

In spite of such long business hours, he managed to see her for a short time almost every day. Sometimes in the early mornings they walked in the small park nearby. Other times they had late-night coffee together, either in his apartment or hers.

On weekends, if he could spare the time, they shared a simple meal and a bottle of wine.

One weekend, when they'd planned to take a short trip upstate, he said regretfully, 'I'm sorry, honey, but I can't make it after all. I have commitments both Saturday and Sunday.'

Faced with yet another lonely weekend, she protested, 'Why do you have to put in such long hours?'

He answered carefully, 'The real estate and property development business is a very demanding one.'

'But surely no one normally works every evening and weekends as well?'

'A great deal of my business is done socially rather than

over a desk, and prospective clients expect me to be available for them twenty-four hours a day, seven days a week.'

Taking her hand, he gave it a squeeze. 'It won't always be like this, I promise you. But at the moment I have no choice.'

Sighing, she accepted the inevitable and, with her usual good sense, agreed, 'Then, I'll just have to make the best of it.'

The following Saturday morning, he appeared unexpectedly at her door. Sounding jubilant, he said, 'You know I've been having talks with your boss?'

Sera nodded. He'd mentioned the fact to her and, one day, she'd actually caught a glimpse of him disappearing into Martin Rothwell's office.

'Well, Rothwell has finally agreed to provide the rest of the financial backing I need to go ahead with a big, new development on Broadway.

'On the strength of that, I've decided to play hookey for once. Let's go and have some fun!' He seized her hand.

'B-but I need to get changed, and do something with my hair,' she stammered.

His eyes running over her grey and white striped button-through dress, her flat-heeled sandals, and the black, silky hair tumbling round her shoulders, he said, 'What you've got on will do fine. And I like your hair loose.'

'Where are we going?' she asked as he swept her down the stairs like a prairie wind.

'We're taking the subway to Coney Island.'

Though somewhat run-down and a mere ghost of its former self, colourful Coney Island, with its amusement arcades and fairground rides, was still amazingly alive and vibrant.

To Sera's unjaded palate, the simple seaside pleasures

it offered, and the sight of so many people having fun, were all she could have asked.

Eating hot dogs and sharing a big bag of fries and a can of cola, she and Keir strolled along the boardwalk enjoying the sunshine, the music, the smells and the ambience.

Noticing her sparkling eyes, he asked, 'Does this kind of thing take you back to your childhood?'

Sera shook her head. 'It's the first time I've ever seen anything quite like this,' she admitted.

His level black brows drew together in a frown. 'Tell me about yourself... Apart from the fact that you work for Rothwell, your mother comes from Boston, and you were brought up in England, I know very little about you.'

Never one for talking about herself, she said, a touch awkwardly, 'There's not much to know. I've led a very dull life.'

'Then, tell me all the dull bits, and I'll try not to yawn.'

'I'm sure you won't be interested.'

'And I'm sure I will,' he disagreed firmly. 'You're an odd mixture of shyness and courage, of warmth and reticence. You like people, yet you tend to leave them alone. I can't imagine you're the sort to make bosom friends and confide in them...'

When, made even more uncomfortable by that shrewd summing up, she said nothing, he went on, 'You have a great deal of quiet pride and, while you fail to condemn others, you're very moral.'

'You make me sound terribly stuffy,' she protested.

'Not at all. You're exactly the sort of woman I'd always hoped to find...'

Her heart swelling, she caught her breath as he added, 'And I want to know what made you that way. So, tell me about your childhood. Where were you brought up?'

'In Sussex.'

'What were your mother and father like?'

'I don't know,' she admitted. 'I never really knew them. They died when I was only two.'

'Tough,' he said simply. 'How did it happen?'

'They left me with my paternal grandmother while they went to France on a skiing holiday. It was to have been a second honeymoon. They were killed in an avalanche the first day there.

'Both my parents had been only children and, apart from my father's mother, neither of them had any close relatives.'

'So who brought you up?'

'My grandmother. She didn't want to be saddled with a child at her age, but she was a woman of strong principles and an even stronger sense of duty.

'Nan had been widowed the previous year and there was very little money, so we lived in a kind of genteel poverty.

'Though she was careful never to say so, I knew, in the way that children *do* know, that I was a burden to her.

'She preferred her own company to that of a child, so I was always left very much to my own devices.'

'But you had school friends?'

Her voice matter-of-fact, Sera said, 'I wasn't encouraged to make friends. Nan had always "kept herself to herself" as she put it, and didn't see why I shouldn't do the same.'

'It must have been very lonely for you.'

'I had some imaginary friends and, thanks to a kindergarten teacher who took an interest in me, I learnt to read at a very early age...'

Seeing the bleak look on Keir's face and worried in case she'd given the wrong impression, Sera added hastily, 'I don't mean Nan was ever unkind to me, and she did everything she was able to do. She insisted on me going to university and, though I lived at home to save money, it was still a struggle to find the fares to travel.

'When I graduated with a first class honours degree and went to work for Anglo American, she was as proud as a peacock and declared the struggle had been well worth it.'

'What did she think of you coming to the States?'

'She never knew. Nan was getting very old and infirm, and she died last winter. Otherwise I wouldn't have left her.

'Her death was one of the reasons I took the chance of a year in New York. The lease on the house was up, and there was nothing to keep me in England...'

For a while they walked in silence, each busy with their thoughts, while music and laughter, the noise of the amusements, and the shrill voices of children, flowed around them.

Then, their casual meal finished, they paused to wipe their greasy fingers on paper napkins, which they disposed of in the nearest litter bin, before strolling on.

Tucking her hand companionably through his arm, Keir asked, 'Now which shall we sample first? The fairground or the aquarium?'

Just happy to be with him, she said, 'I don't mind in the slightest. It's up to you.'

'In that case, let's go for all the fun of the fair.'

As though trying to make up for her colourless child-hood, Keir pulled out all the stops and the rest of the day was packed with more pleasure and excitement than Sera had known in the whole of her life.

When, her face glowing, she thanked him, he said with an odd kind of tenderness, 'At the moment you're easy to please, my love.'

Hot, tired, and dusty, but completely happy, they were heading back to the subway when some jewellery being displayed by a street vendor caught Sera's eye and she paused to take a second look.

The item that had attracted her attention was a narrow silver ring with an unusual chased design.

'Seen something you fancy?' Keir queried, reaching for his wallet.

If it had been anything but a ring, she might have told him. As it was...

Flushing a little, she shook her head and made to move on.

'How about this as a memento?' As though he had second sight, he reached to pick up the very ring she'd been looking at. 'Try it on.'

When she hesitated, he took her left hand and slipped it on to her engagement finger. 'That fits quite well.'

Turning to the vendor, who was sporting dreadlocks and a plaited headband, he asked, 'How much?'

Moving a wad of gum from one side of his mouth to the other, the man weighed up Keir and, apparently deciding not to push it, suggested, 'Twenty dollars?'

Keir nodded and the money changed hands.

As they walked away, Keir's arm round Sera's waist, he murmured, *sotto voce*, 'It might be as well not to keep it on too long. It will probably turn your finger green.'

Lifting her hand to look at it, she said, 'I'll chance that.'

He gave her a squeeze. 'One day, hopefully in the not too distant future, I'll buy you something a great deal more expensive from Tiffany's.'

A feeling of pure joy and thankfulness filled her. Keir loved her and wanted to marry her.

No matter what he bought her in the future, nothing could ever take the place of this ring and she would never be happier than she was at this moment...

CHAPTER TWO

IT WAS almost eleven o'clock when they reached the Brownstone and climbed the stairs. Sensing that he was about to leave her at her door and not wanting this magic day to end, Sera asked quickly, 'Won't you come in for a coffee?'

Looking into eyes unconsciously pleading, he agreed, 'So long as it's a quick one. I'll need an early start in the morning to make up for today.'

She made two mugs of instant and they drank them sitting side by side on the couch that, with its brightly patterned duvet, was also a bed.

As soon as the mugs were empty he rose to go and Sera accompanied him to the door.

Until today, he had, intentionally it seemed, kept things very casual, a handclasp, a brotherly hug, a peck on the cheek.

Now, when he bent his dark head, with innocent boldness, she lifted her lips for his kiss. After the briefest of hesitations, his mouth brushed hers.

The lightest touch, but it proved to be as explosive as dropping a lighted match into a keg of gunpowder.

Without conscious volition, her lips parted beneath that light pressure and, making a sound almost like a groan, he gathered her into his arms and began to kiss her deeply.

Head whirling, she clung to him, while his hands started to move over her body, tracing her slim waist and the curve of her hip and buttock, before moving up to find the soft swell of her breast.

When those skilful fingers began to tease the sensitive nipple, she was shaken by shudders of delight and the kind of fierce desire she had never dreamt existed.

Knowing all about sex in theory, if not in fact, she had naively supposed that love and sex would go hand in hand to produce a mutual *manageable* pleasure. She had never visualized being swept away by such extremes of passion.

When, with a sudden urgency, he began to undo the buttons of her dress and the front fastening of her bra, she would have helped him, but her hands were shaking too much.

Tossing the garments aside, he stooped to nuzzle his face against her breasts, taking first one nipple into his mouth and then the other.

The pleasure was so pure, so exquisite, that she thought she could stand no more when, kneeling at her feet, he began to ease off her dainty briefs, kissing his way down her flat belly until he reached the tangle of black silky curls.

A kind of sensual overload made her give a little gasping cry.

Getting to his feet, he said thickly, 'It's all right, my love. It's all right.'

Suddenly desperately afraid he was going to walk away and leave her, she threw her arms around his neck and, her mouth finding his and clinging to it, pressed herself against him.

For a split second he seemed to hold back. Then, to her utmost relief, he began to kiss her again. After a moment he stooped and, lifting her effortlessly in his arms, carried her back to the couch and laid her down on top of the duvet.

Her heart pounding, her mouth dry, she watched him

strip off his own clothes and, when he came to her, she welcomed him with open arms.

In spite of his own urgency, he was a gentle, considerate lover, skilful and generous. He made her first experience of physical love a beautiful experience, one she knew she would always remember with wonder and delight.

When his dark head lay heavy on her breast, stroking his curly hair, she was filled with such love and tenderness, such joy, that, unable to contain so much emotion, her heart found an outlet in tears.

Her mood of ecstasy was so all-embracing that it had never occurred to her that Keir might not feel the same.

It took her completely by surprise when, lifting himself away, he said in a queer, shaken voice, 'I'm sorry. I never meant this to happen, believe me...' Then sharply, 'Did I hurt you?'

'No, of course not.' She smiled at him tremulously.

'Then, why are you crying?'

'I'm just so *happy*. Please tell me *you* are. I couldn't bear it if you were disappointed.'

'Of course I'm happy.' He raised her hand to his lips and kissed the palm, before saying soberly, 'I just hope to goodness I can keep things that way.'

At that moment, still euphoric, she could think of no reason why they shouldn't both be happy for the rest of their lives.

Swinging his feet to the floor, he sat on the edge of the couch, his dark head bent as though in thought.

She was admiring the elegant line of his spine, the clear, healthy skin, the width of his shoulders, when something about the tenseness of his neck muscles made her ask. 'Is something wrong?'

'I'm a damned fool.' Swinging round to face her, he added with sudden violence, 'You were a virgin...'

'That's true.' Her lovely, humorous, self-derisive smile flashed out. 'But being a virgin isn't a crime. And I didn't want to stay a virgin for ever.'

Heavily, without hope, he queried, 'I take it you're not protected?'

'As a matter of fact, I am.' Smiling a little at his astonished face, she said, 'My doctor suggested I went on the pill for a minor hormone imbalance.'

She heard his sigh of unutterable relief.

Gently, she asked, 'Would it have mattered so *very* much if I hadn't been?'

'Yes, it would,' he answered shortly.

Sera was dismayed. 'Then, you don't like children?'

'Of course I like children. But this is no time to be getting you pregnant.'

Perhaps not, as they weren't married yet. But as they loved each other, it wouldn't have been the end of the world.

Rising to his feet, he eased the light duvet free and pulled it over her. But instead of getting back into bed, as she'd hoped, he began to put on his clothes.

As he shrugged into his shirt, she asked, 'Do you have to go?'

Keir heard the sudden desolation and, coming back to sit on the edge of the bed, he stroked her cheek with a gentle finger. 'I'm afraid so.'

'But *why*?'

'Because I shouldn't have let this happen. The time isn't right. If it was just a casual affair, with no commitment on either side, it wouldn't be a problem. But it isn't. And it's too soon.

'At the moment I need every single minute, and every scrap of energy and concentration I can muster.' Then, with a sigh he added, 'I can only ask you to be patient.'

Sera nodded wordlessly. She could, and *would*, do anything Keir wanted her to do.

'That's my girl.' He kissed the tip of her nose, switched off the light and, a second later, she heard the door close quietly behind him.

Lying staring blindly into the darkness, she thought long and deeply about Keir's reaction to their lovemaking, while any remaining euphoria faded slowly away.

She couldn't regret what had happened, it had been so beautiful, so *right*...

Only Keir hadn't thought so; he hadn't really wanted it to happen. And, with hindsight, she could see that he'd been a reluctant lover. She had sensed his attempt to hold back.

Afterwards he'd said he was happy, but his words had lacked conviction. Perhaps he'd only said it because she'd pressed him...

But he *had* wanted her. Inexperienced though she was, there had been no mistaking his hunger and need. And he *did* love her. She felt for the ring he'd placed on her finger, and was reassured.

All it amounted to, she told herself firmly, was that, with the amount of work he was trying to get done, there was no time at the present for a wife and a family.

As he himself had said, it was too soon.

But for a man who was as much of a workaholic as he was, would there ever be time?

No, she mustn't think like that. If she was patient as he'd asked, surely everything would come right?

Sunday was a long, lonely day, and by ten-thirty that evening Sera had given up all hope of Keir coming. She had cleaned her teeth and put on a thin cotton nightdress, when there was the lightest of taps at the door.

Hurrying over, she threw it open.

'Hi.' He smiled at her. 'I wondered if you might be asleep.'

Her relief and pleasure at seeing him was so great that, for a moment, she was speechless.

Then, because she couldn't say all the things she felt, she asked mundanely, 'Are you coming in for a coffee?'

He shook his head. 'I just wanted to make sure you were all right.'

Anxious not to pressure him, she said brightly, 'I'm fine.'

Her reward was a light kiss on the cheek. 'Then, I'll see you tomorrow morning at six-thirty. We'll have a walk in the park, weather permitting. If it's raining—'

Afraid of what he was going to say, she broke in hurriedly, 'If it's raining, I'll cook you some breakfast.'

Grinning, he said, 'When I say my prayers, I'll pray for rain.'

Back on their former footing, snatching whatever time together he could manage, the next couple of weeks were happy ones for Sera.

Though Keir never made any attempt to make love to her, and kept the relationship light, there was a warmth about him, a caring that spoke volumes.

At odd times, when he looked at her, she saw desire flare in those long, heavy-lidded eyes.

Desire that lit an answering flame.

Had he made the slightest move, she would have gone to him willingly, eagerly. But, always with a will-power she could only marvel at, he beat it down.

The fact that he refused to take what she would happily have given, served only to deepen her feelings for him.

Love, as a poet once said, is hard to hide, and there was a glow about her that lit up the office.

Returning from a business trip, Cheryl Rothwell noticed that radiance, and remarked to her PA, 'You look as if life's giving you a treat.' Then, shrewdly she added, 'Which means a man. What's his name?'

Taken by surprise, Sera found herself admitting, 'Keir Sutherlands.'

'Keir Sutherlands?' Cheryl sounded startled, and none too pleased. 'Some man!'

Though she smiled, Sera could sense the unspoken envy.

Her expression interested, Cheryl observed, 'I met him a couple of weeks ago when Martin and he had some business to discuss...'

All at once she paused, her attention caught by the silver ring Sera wore. But after a moment's scrutiny, clearly dismissing it as of no importance, she went on, 'Though I wouldn't call him film-star handsome, he's an attractive devil, and his sex appeal hits you like a sock on the jaw.'

Then, sharply, she asked, 'Where did *you* meet him? Was it here?'

'No. He has an apartment next door to mine.'

Cheryl frowned. 'What's a man who owns Sutherlands doing living in some run-down apartment building?'

Sera, who had never considered the question, shook her head.

'Do you know how long he's lived there?' Cheryl pursued.

'Only for a short time, I gather.'

'Odd... Perhaps I'll ask him about it when he comes to the party on Thursday night...'

Anglo American did a great deal of corporate entertaining. Like Keir, Martin Rothwell considered that more opportunities presented themselves and more real business was done in a relaxed, social atmosphere than over an office desk.

Her light blue eyes on her PA's face, Cheryl added casually, 'I suppose you'll be coming?'

Well aware that it wasn't the answer the other woman was hoping for, Sera said steadily, 'Yes, Keir said he'd take me.'

But, sounding more like herself, Cheryl exclaimed, 'Lucky you! I can't say I'm not jealous.'

When Keir finally knocked at Sera's door on Thursday evening he was well over an hour late, and she had practically given him up.

Brushing his apology aside, she assured him, 'It doesn't matter. Honestly. Posh parties really aren't my thing.'

'How many have you been to?'

'None,' she admitted.

'Then I'll do my best to see you enjoy this one.'

He was looking devastatingly attractive in well-cut evening clothes and, knowing this gathering was certain to be a lavish affair, she asked a shade hesitantly, 'Will I do?'

She had splashed out on a new dress, and with only a limited amount to spend had gone for simplicity, choosing a slim-fitting ankle-length sheath in muted shades of green and dull silver.

'Not everyone can wear this kind of thing,' the sales girl had remarked, 'but you sure have the figure for it.'

Sera's only reservation had been the scooped neckline, which revealed the soft swell of her breasts and more than a glimpse of cleavage.

She was wearing her only piece of jewellery, a long, thin, silver chain that looped twice. It had been her mother's, and she had worn it ever since her grandmother had given it to her for her eighteenth birthday.

Keir's glance travelling slowly over her, from her elegant knot of hair to her matching sandals. He raised her hand to his lips. 'My love, you look enchanting,' he said huskily.

Thrilled by the endearment, she asked, 'You don't think the neckline's too daring?'

'No...' His eyes on the longest loop of the chain, which disappeared into her cleavage, he added ruefully, 'Though it's daring enough to raise my blood pressure several notches.'

Seeing the lick of flame in his dark blue eyes, she waited, hoping he would suggest staying at home. When he didn't, she said prosaically, 'If we're going on the subway, I'd better get a coat.'

He shook his head. 'You won't need one. It's a hot night, and all this finery calls for a taxi.'

When they reached the Plaza Hotel, off Fifth Avenue, the party was in full swing. People were standing in groups sipping champagne while they laughed and talked, and the air was filled with the scent of French perfume and the sweet smell of success.

Glancing around the large, handsome room at the assembled company, Sera saw that nearly all the women were dressed in top designer clothes and displaying enough precious stones to fill Aladdin's cave. While the men, along with their immaculate evening clothes, wore that unmistakable air of confidence and authority that wealth brings.

Though knowing herself to be underdressed, with her off-the-peg sheath and simple chain, Sera held her head high. While Keir was by her side, she was well content.

She might be out of place in this glittering throng, but *he* certainly wasn't.

He was a man who could, without effort, establish moral ascendancy over his peers, easily holding his own amongst the rich and powerful, and several covert glances told her that a lot of the women there envied her of her escort.

She found herself wishing that she could have fitted in better for his sake; she didn't want him to feel ashamed of her.

As though guessing her feelings, he tucked her hand through his arm and, with calm assurance, led her over to their host and hostess.

Cheryl, her red-gold hair like a shining helmet, was wearing a dramatic dress of shimmering jade green. She had all the striking gauntness of a model, and there were diamonds around her neck and in her ears.

Her brother, looking relaxed and debonair, was impressive in immaculate evening clothes.

Though she had worked in the same set of offices for some weeks now, Sera had never actually met Martin Rothwell, only catching a distant glimpse of him from time to time.

She knew he was in his early thirties, a year younger than Cheryl, who had once playfully described him as 'my baby brother'.

At close quarters he looked even younger and, seeing brother and sister standing together, Sera realized for the first time how very alike they were.

Both were tall and well-built, with the kind of red-gold hair that was often called ginger—though Cheryl's was several shades darker than her brother's. They both had pale blue eyes, the kind of skin that freckles easily, a short nose, and a long upper lip.

There, the resemblance ended.

Martin Rothwell had a rather heavy face with flat cheeks

and a squarish jaw, while Cheryl's face was a smooth oval with prominent cheekbones.

They were very good-looking in their own way, and Martin had the reputation of being a charmer where women were concerned.

'Sutherlands, glad you could make it,' he said expansively, and held out his hand.

Watching them together, Sera noticed that, though Keir was a good six feet and broad-shouldered, Martin was equally tall and considerably heavier.

The two men shook hands. Neither smiled.

'You've met my sister, of course?'

'Miss Rothwell,' Keir murmured politely, taking the proffered hand.

'Oh, *Cheryl*, please.'

Turning to her brother, whose light eyes were fixed on Sera's exquisite face, Cheryl said, 'I don't think you've actually met Sera Reynolds, my new PA? Sera's only been here a few weeks. She's from the London branch.'

'I can see I've been missing out.' Taking her hand, Martin smiled at her and, all at once, Sera could see *why* he had that reputation for charm.

His clasp was cool and firm and he held her hand rather longer than was strictly necessary before releasing it.

By her side, she sensed rather than felt, Keir stiffen slightly, and saw by the gleam in Martin's eye that he had noticed and was pleased by that instinctive reaction.

The men might do business together, she realized, but they were far from liking one another.

Smiling a little, Martin asked blandly, 'So, how are you settling in, Sera?'

'Quite well, I think.'

'And you like New York?'

'Oh, yes.'

'Have you had a chance to see much of it?'

Before Sera could answer, Cheryl gave her brother a swift, conspiratorial glance and, stepping forward, slid her hand through Keir's arm.

'If you can spare a few minutes, there's someone I think you should meet. His name is Roberto Canelli. Though I only met him myself a few days ago, I happen to know he's been looking for a suitable site to relocate his business.'

Turning to Sera, Keir asked, 'I hope you don't mind?'

Well aware that business was the be all and the end all of the evening, she answered valiantly, 'No, of course not.'

He gave her a swift, grateful smile and promised, 'I'll try not to be too long.'

'Canelli's about to complete a deal with Bensons,' Cheryl warned, 'so if you have anything that might interest him, you'll have to move fast...'

A moment later, feeling rather lost, Sera watched as they walked away and disappeared into the throng.

Cheryl was very tall for a woman, almost six feet in her high heels, and with their two heads close together, one so smooth and bright, the other so dark and curly, they made a handsome couple.

'As you've just arrived, you won't have eaten yet?' Martin's voice broke into Sera's thoughts.

'No,' she admitted.

'Then, while we get to know each other, shall we go and see what the buffet has to offer?' A hand at her waist, he led her through to the adjoining room.

As she might have expected, the tables held an excellent and varied selection of food, while above the hum of conversation glasses clinked and champagne corks popped.

With a gallantry she found slightly embarrassing, Martin

insisted on helping her to a selection of hors d'oeuvres before serving himself.

A lot of the top men from the world of finance were gathered by the buffet, standing in little groups of twos and threes, making new contacts and cementing old ones over smoked salmon canapés and glasses of vintage champagne.

While they ate, Martin pointed out several whose names were synonymous with wealth and power, and told her amusing anecdotes about each.

Sera was laughing at one of them when Keir appeared at her side. She turned to him eagerly.

His expression curiously tight, he told her, 'Signor Canelli is interested in a site near SoHo that's just recently come on the market. He'd like to take a look at it straight away, so Cheryl has kindly offered to drive us down there. Will you be all right?'

Her heart dropping like a lead weight, Sera said, 'I'll be fine.' Then trying not to sound anxious, 'Have you any idea how long you'll be?'

'It'll depend on the traffic, I'm afraid.' Giving her hand a squeeze, he assured her, 'But I'll be as quick as I can.'

'If you don't happen to make it back,' Martin said smoothly, 'I'll see Sera gets home safely.'

'Thank you, but I expect to *be* back.' Keir's voice was only just civil.

It was obvious that he wasn't happy about leaving her with Martin Rothwell. But business came first.

His face set, he turned and walked away.

Treating the other man's reappearance as an unwanted intrusion, Martin asked cheerfully, 'Now then, where were we?'

For the next twenty minutes or so, while they stood by

the buffet, he plied her with delicacies and, though he himself drank little, made sure her glass was kept topped up.

Giving her his undivided attention, he asked her a string of questions. Where did she live...? What did she like most about New York...? How did she think life in the States compared with life in England?

He seemed genuinely interested in her answers, and she found him surprisingly easy to talk to.

One of his comments made her ask, 'Do you know England well?'

'Fairly well. We have English ancestry and both Cheryl and I have spent some time over there. After leaving college I lived in London for almost three years...'

Despite his charm, he was known to be a hard-headed businessman, and Sera expected him to excuse himself as soon as the meal was over, rather than waste any more time on one of his own employees.

But, even when they'd finished eating and their coffee cups were empty, he remained by her side.

Aware that he would need to mingle with his guests, she put down her cup and said politely, 'Thank you, Mr Rothwell, that was most enjoyable,' and made to leave him.

'Don't go...' he put a restraining hand on her arm '...and out of the office please call me Martin.' Seeing the look on her face, he said teasingly, 'Go on, try it. It's not that difficult. *Martin.*'

'Martin,' she echoed uncertainly.

'Not bad. All you need is a little more practice.'

His hand lingered on her arm as he queried, 'As you've been in New York such a short time you can't know many people here?'

'No.'

'Then let me introduce you to a few.'

'I'm afraid I'm not really dressed for it.'

His pale blue eyes on her face, he said, 'As far as I'm concerned, you're quite perfect.'

Disconcerted, she stammered, 'Th-thank you, but Keir might be back soon, and I—'

'If he does turn up, I'll reluctantly hand you over. Until then, let's circulate.'

He offered her his arm and, feeling she had no option, she took it.

Uncomfortable at first, after a while and rather to her surprise, Sera began to relax and enjoy a novel experience.

On the arm of the big boss, she found herself being regarded with a kind of deference and respect that made her smile inwardly.

As they moved from group to group, pausing to talk to what Martin termed the 'more interesting' of his guests, he introduced her simply as 'Miss Reynolds, an English colleague.'

When the conversation invariably turned to the current financial scene, with a flattering certainty that she knew what she was talking about, he drew her into each discussion, inviting her opinion and treating her as an equal.

It was heady stuff.

An evening she'd only looked forward to because Keir was taking her became stimulating and enjoyable, despite his continued absence.

Towards eleven, people began to drift away, and she found herself saying goodnight to Martin's guests as though she was his hostess.

The party was coming to an end, with still no sign of either Cheryl or Keir. Oh, what on earth was keeping them? she wondered.

Apparently interpreting her anxious expression, Martin said, 'It doesn't look as if they're going to get back.'

'No.' The monosyllable sounded forlorn, when she'd meant it to sound matter-of-fact.

'In that case, I'll be happy to see you home.'

Knowing he and his sister shared an apartment on Fifth Avenue, she refused hastily. 'Thank you, but there's really no need for you to go out of your way.'

As though she hadn't spoken, he asked, 'Where do you live?'

She told him, adding firmly, 'I can easily get a taxi.'

'I won't hear of it. A promise is a promise. And you've been neglected enough for one night.'

Not by him, she hadn't. Though she was a mere employee and he the host of a party thrown solely for business reasons, Martin had contrived to put her interests before business.

Whereas Keir...

Though she immediately snapped off the disloyal thought, a faint feeling of resentment was born.

A hand beneath her elbow, Martin queried, 'Have you a wrap?'

She shook her head.

'Then, let's go.'

When she had been handed into his silver-grey, chauffeur-driven limousine, Martin climbed in beside her and asked, 'Have you discovered New York by night?'

'Not really.' She had spent most evenings sitting in her room, waiting in case Keir might call.

'Then you must see Times Square and the lights on Broadway.'

Sliding aside the glass panel, Martin gave the chauffeur her address, adding, 'Drive down Broadway, will you, Carlson?'

To Sera, he explained, 'Broadway follows an old Indian

trail, so it's the one street that mars Midtown Manhattan's perfect grid system...'

During the journey he pointed out things of interest and talked easily, entertainingly, about the New York scene and the current musicals.

'I take it you haven't been to a Broadway production yet?' he queried.

'No, but I'm certainly hoping to. Is it difficult to get tickets?'

'That depends on what you'd like to see.'

She named one of the latest shows, and was totally disconcerted when he said, 'I'll see what I can do.'

'Oh, but I—I didn't mean—'

Leaning over, he put a finger to her lips. 'I know you didn't. But it will be my pleasure.'

When they reached the Brownstone on Quarles Street, Martin got out with her.

A quick glance at the top floor showed that Keir's window was still dark. So he wasn't home yet.

Remembering Cheryl's obvious interest in him, Sera felt slightly uneasy. She had discovered almost at once that, where men were concerned, the redhead was unashamedly predatory...

She became aware that Martin was standing waiting and held out her hand, saying formally, 'Thank you for everything. You've been more than kind.'

He took her hand and tucked it under his arm. 'I'll see you up.'

'But I live on the top floor and there's no lift.'

'Do I look that decrepit?' he asked quizzically.

'Of course not, but there really isn't any need.'

'Let me be the judge of that.'

He accompanied her up the steps and, when she'd let herself in, followed her across the brown-linoleum-covered hall and up the five flights of stairs, where traces of the evening's cooking smells—greens, onions, garlic, pastrami—still lingered on the hot, stale air.

Turning to glance at him, she saw his nose wrinkle. 'How on earth do you manage in a place like this?' he asked with distaste.

'It's not really so bad,' she defended the Brownstone. 'In fact, I'm quite enjoying living here.'

She refrained from adding that, when Keir was with her, it was as close to heaven as she was every likely to get.

'Didn't personnel give you any help?' Martin questioned.

'Yes. They went to a great deal of trouble.'

'It doesn't look like it to me. I'll have to see if they can't come up with something better.'

'Prices in New York are high,' she pointed out quietly. 'I couldn't *afford* anything better.'

For a moment he looked angry and she realized that, when he'd set his mind on something, he wasn't used to being thwarted.

Then he shrugged and suggested with a smile, 'In that case, you'll have to try asking Cheryl for an increase in salary.'

When they reached her door, Sera thanked him again. 'I really am very grateful for everything.'

His pale blue eyes on her face, he suggested, 'In that case, there's something you can do for me.'

Watching her freeze, he told her crisply, 'No, it's not what you're thinking. When I *do* take you to bed, the last thing I'll be looking for is *gratitude*, believe me.'

'I—I'm sorry,' she stammered, feeling foolish. 'What is it you want me to do?'

'Tomorrow I'm having lunch with Ralph Kessler and

his wife. It's part social and part business. Cheryl, who usually joins me on these occasions, is tied up.

'I need someone with me who's intelligent enough to cope with the business side if they both want to talk business, and pleasant enough to carry off the social side if Mrs Kessler just wants to talk. In other words, I'd like you to act as my hostess.'

'I'd be happy to,' she agreed, still kicking herself for her previous blunder. Then hesitantly she said, 'But I really haven't anything suitable to wear.'

He brushed that off as an excuse. 'Don't worry, wear anything. Oh, and don't bother to go into the office in the morning. I'll pick you up here at about eleven.' Then coolly he said, 'Goodnight, Sera.'

'Goodnight,' she answered and, in something of a daze, watched him turn and descend the stairs two at a time.

She had been subconsciously on her guard, half expecting him to try to kiss her, her instincts telling her that, despite knowing about Keir, he had more than a boss/employee relationship in mind.

But perhaps, lacking experience in such matters, she'd totally misread things?

Then recalling his, 'When I *do* take you to bed...' she knew her instincts had been right.

Well, it was only a business lunch she'd committed herself to and, from now on, she'd be doubly careful.

While she took off her make-up and cleaned her teeth in the tiny cramped bathroom, she listened for any sounds of Keir returning, but heard nothing.

When she finally donned her nightie and got into bed she left her light on, hoping that when he did come he would know she was awake, and knock.

CHAPTER THREE

W<small>HEN</small> Sera surfaced slowly, reluctantly, her light was still on, but made tawdry by the sunshine filtering through the curtains. She felt disturbed and anxious without knowing precisely why.

It took a minute for her head to clear enough to recall the previous night. It had been after two before she'd fallen into an exhausted sleep and, still, Keir hadn't returned.

Glancing at the simple watch she wore on a plain black strap, she saw that it was almost ten-thirty, and Martin was coming to pick her up at eleven.

Stumbling out of bed, she pulled on her dressing gown and, leaving her own door slightly ajar, went to knock on Keir's.

There was no answer. Had he been and gone? Or hadn't he returned at all?

But even someone as dedicated as he didn't work all night. So what *had* he been doing?

Unbidden, a picture of Cheryl's striking face and body flashed into Sera's mind.

With a sudden pang she remembered what Keir had said after they had made love. 'If it was just a casual affair, with no commitment on either side, it wouldn't be a problem…'

At the time she hadn't thought about his words too closely, hadn't envisaged that he might apply them in other ways.

He'd made no promises about being faithful to her, and

she'd asked for none. She had simply thought that, if he loved her, everything would be all right.

But would it?

Cheryl had more than enough sex appeal to light up Broadway, and very few scruples. If she made it plain that she fancied him...well, Keir was a red-blooded man...

Heart-sick, Sera turned away from his door and hurried back to her own room to shower and get ready for when Martin arrived.

Catching sight of herself in the spotted mirror, Sera saw she looked pale and depressed, and made herself up with care before coiling her black silky hair into a smooth knot.

Having nothing more suitable, she put on a white blouse, a charcoal-grey skirt and jacket, and grey leather court shoes. She had just picked up her bag when there was a knock at the door.

Perhaps it was Keir.

She rushed to open it and was disappointed to find Martin standing there.

Seeing the light die out of her face, he asked shrewdly, 'Were you expecting someone else?'

'No.'

He quirked a sandy brow. 'Then, you don't like my tie?'

Making an effort, she answered lightly, 'On the contrary, I love it.'

'In that case, I may never change it.'

Watching twin dimples appear as she smiled, he asked, 'Ready to go?'

Indicating her suit, she queried, 'Will this do?'

He pursed his lips. 'It's smart, but too office-like for this kind of semi-social occasion.'

'I'm afraid I don't have anything more suitable.'

'That can soon be remedied. We'll stop off at Barron Conté.'

'No,' she said sharply.

His pale blue eyes turned cold. 'We would be merely purchasing the right clothes for the job. If you were an office cleaner and the company supplied you with an overall, I take it you would have no objections?'

'No, but—'

'This is a matter of business. You're doing a job for the company for which you'll get paid and for which you need to be stylishly dressed. You don't *have* to keep the clothes if you don't want to.'

She bit her lip. Perhaps this kind of thing was the norm? Maybe she was making a fuss about nothing?

'What do you say?'

'Very well,' she agreed unwillingly. 'If there's enough time.'

'There'll be plenty of time.' He smiled his satisfaction. 'We're not meeting the Kesslers until one o'clock.'

If lunch wasn't until one, why had he come to pick her up so early? Unless he'd had this in mind from the start?

Suddenly, recalling how last night he'd said 'Don't worry, wear anything', she knew he *had*, and felt a sudden apprehension, a growing suspicion that she was being *manipulated*.

'Buy whatever you need,' Martin ordered when they reached Barron Conté and dropped Sera off, 'and charge it to the company. Price is no object.'

Warily she asked, 'But what *kind* of thing would be most suitable?'

'I'll leave that to your good taste. But get a complete outfit, including undies.'

Not on your life, she thought. Buying undies had an implication that was unacceptable. The only clothes and accessories she was prepared to buy were the ones that would be *visible* and were strictly necessary.

'Now I've some business to see to. I'll pick you up in about an hour,' Martin added.

Some fifty minutes later, her own clothes packed in a black and gold striped box, Sera emerged from the famous Fifth Avenue store and climbed into the waiting limousine.

She was still dressed in a suit, but the cut, the design, and the raw silk made it a far cry from the one that she had been wearing.

His glance running over her, Martin said with undisguised admiration, 'You look a million dollars...'

With the sheerest of stockings and a pair of handmade shoes, she *felt* a million dollars.

'Though I'd prefer it if you didn't wear *this*. It doesn't go with the outfit.' Before she could guess his intention, he picked up her left hand and, slipping off her ring, dropped it into his pocket.

Sera held out her hand, saying as levelly as possible, 'I'd like my ring back, please.'

Seeing the angry sparkle in her green eyes, he retrieved the ring and dropped it into her waiting palm.

'Thank you.' She put it carefully into her purse.

'Not an engagement ring, surely?' he enquired.

'A memento...' Wasn't that what Keir had called it? *She* had thought of it as an engagement ring but, looking back, she knew Keir hadn't. All he'd said was, 'It might be as well not to keep it on too long. It will probably turn your finger green.'

And, when she'd told him she would chance it, he'd added, 'One day, hopefully in the not too distant future, I'll buy you something a great deal more expensive from Tiffany's.'

A casual promise to be kept or ignored.

Nothing binding, whatever she'd read into it.

'Just a memento.' Though her voice wasn't quite steady, she managed a smile.

Their destination proved to be Rands, a quiet, exclusive restaurant just off Madison Avenue. They had been waiting in the foyer for only a short time when Martin's guests arrived.

Ralph Kessler was a quiet, unassuming man, while his wife, a plump, well-dressed blonde, proved to be friendly and garrulous.

As soon as the two men settled down to a business discussion, Amy Kessler began to talk about clothes. 'I just love your suit,' she said admiringly. 'The material's beautiful and I simply *adore* that shade of lilac.'

She was explaining in detail what colours suited her best and how she coordinated her wardrobe, when Sera, happening to glance up, froze.

Sitting across the room, at a table for two, were Cheryl and Keir. Though they were partly shielded by an ornate grille, there was no mistaking that dark, well-shaped head and the bright, red-gold one.

They were leaning towards each other, talking intimately, and while Sera watched, feeling as if she was slowly bleeding to death, Cheryl put out her hand and Keir took it.

Tearing her gaze away, Sera made an effort to focus on Amy Kessler's carefully made-up face, but all she could see was Keir holding Cheryl's hand and gazing into her eyes.

Suddenly realizing that the blonde had stopped talking, and guiltily aware that she hadn't heard a word, Sera took a chance and asked, 'So, do you have a favourite colour, Mrs Kessler?'

'Oh, pink, without a doubt.' Amy was under way again.

'It's such a *flattering* colour. As I keep saying to Ralph, now I'm not twenty any longer...'

When, unable to stop herself, Sera eventually let her eyes stray to the table where Cheryl and Keir had been sitting, it was empty.

As soon as lunch was over, Ralph Kessler excused himself on the grounds that he had a three o'clock meeting. 'It's been most pleasant,' he said cordially.

'Most pleasant,' his wife echoed, beaming at Sera.

'Then, we must do it more often,' Martin said as they all shook hands and the Kesslers departed, arm in arm.

'A very successful meeting,' Martin commented. Pouring Sera and himself more coffee, he added, 'Though you may not think it, Amy Kessler is a shrewd business-woman, while her husband is one of the cleverest men on the stock exchange. He has an unerring instinct for how the market will move, so he's also one of the richest. He once told me that the only reason he bothered to keep making money was that his wife enjoyed spending it.'

'They seem fond of one another.' Her mind on what she'd seen earlier, Sera said the first thing that came into her head.

'I believe they are. They've been married for more than twenty years. Which must be something of a record in this day and age.'

'You sound a shade cynical.'

'My own marriage—admittedly I was young at the time—lasted six months. I was so blinded by Linda's beauty it took me that length of time to realize she was a self-centred little tramp with neither character nor brains.'

Not knowing what to say, Sera finished her coffee in silence.

'Now, what are you doing for the rest of the day?' Martin asked as he rose to pull out her chair.

'I'm going straight to the office. I can get changed there and—'

Martin shook his head. 'It's almost two-thirty. I can't see the point of going in so late on a Friday afternoon.'

'Oh, but Miss Rothwell might—'

'Cheryl won't be there. She was coming to Pine Cove with me, but I had a brief word with her earlier and she told me she has other plans for the weekend... Her latest man, I gather,' he added casually as they crossed the foyer. 'They're going to have a romantic away-from-it-all break in the Catskills.'

Shock hit Sera like a blow to the solar plexus and she was forced to sit down abruptly on one of the gilt chairs.

Her heart seemed to have stopped beating and her lungs refused to function. She felt as though she couldn't breathe, as though she was suffocating.

After making it clear that he had no time for a relationship with *her*, Keir was taking Cheryl away for the weekend.

Of course, it would be different, Sera reminded herself bitterly, a purely physical thing between two sophisticated people. The kind of non-relationship that Keir had said wouldn't be a problem.

There would be no need for any kind of commitment, no emotional hang-ups. Cheryl would neither ask for, nor expect, more than he was prepared to give...

'Are you all right?' Martin sounded concerned.

She drew a shuddering breath and said as levelly as possible, 'Yes, thank you. I just turned a bit light-headed. It's probably the wine. I'm not used to drinking, especially at lunch-time.'

'You look very pale.'

'I'm fine now.'

'Then, I'll take you home.'

Lacking the spirit to argue, she got to her feet and, praying that her legs would support her, made for the exit.

Right on cue, the silver-grey limousine drew up outside and Carlson jumped out to open the door.

'Have you any plans for the weekend?' Martin asked as he got in beside her.

'No,' she said baldly.

His pale blue eyes, with their sandy lashes, on her face, he suggested, 'How would you like to come with me to Long Island? I have a house at the Hamptons. The forecast is for a good weekend, so we could make full use of the beach, or laze by the pool if you'd prefer it?'

Seeing her stiffen, he said, 'No, I'm not proposing a spot of lust in the sun. I'm simply inviting you to join a weekend house party at Pine Cove. Cheryl has cried off, so there'll be a woman short...'

Social gatherings weren't her thing at the best of times... And how could she bear to join a house party, feeling as though she was bleeding to death inside?

'You won't even need to speak to me if you don't want to,' Martin added humorously. 'There'll be another four or five couples, all young and all good company...'

That would simply be turning the screw. Seeing other couples happy together would make it almost impossible to hide all her own pain and misery...

Watching her face and seeing she was about to refuse, he pressed, 'Why not give it a whirl? You have no plans for the weekend, so what have you got to lose?'

What *had* she got to lose?

Put like that, the answer was, absolutely nothing.

She could imagine little pleasure in going, but wouldn't the alternative be even worse? If she didn't go she would end up sitting alone, picturing Keir in the arms of another woman.

It would be torture.

Making up her mind in a rush, she said, 'Thank you. I'd like to come.'

Though it was swiftly hidden, she saw the flare of excitement and triumph that blazed across Martin's face.

'Good! Then we'll stop off at your apartment so you can pick up whatever you need. If you don't bother to get changed, how long will it take you to pack?'

'Just a few minutes.' Her answer was reluctant.

'Then we can be on the Long Island Expressway before the traffic builds up...'

Now she had committed herself, with Martin's look of elation fresh in her mind, Sera was having second thoughts. Already aware that he was interested in her, she should have had the sense to refuse his invitation.

She would have preferred to retain a purely businesslike relationship, to regard Martin Rothwell simply as her boss.

Her private life had just disintegrated around her, and the last thing she wanted was for her working life to be complicated by his unwanted interest.

Sighing inwardly, she decided that, over the weekend, if he showed any signs of getting too friendly, she would have to make it quite plain that she had no intention of indulging in an affair, or a fling, or whatever he had in mind.

In the event, Sera couldn't fault his behaviour. He made no attempt to get her alone or pressure her in any way, but treated her with the same kind of cheerful *bonhomie* that he treated his other guests.

All the other couples proved to be friendly and, as

Martin had said, good company. If Sera hadn't felt so desolate, the weekend would have been enjoyable.

As it was, she prayed for Sunday evening to come so she could be alone and lick her wounds in private.

Good weather encouraging them to linger by the pool, they made a late start back. The traffic was heavy and it was getting on for ten o'clock when they drew up outside the Brownstone.

As the chauffeur produced her small weekend case, Sera glanced up at Keir's unlit window. It appeared he wasn't yet home.

Martin got out with her, but this time, to her relief, he made no move to accompany her inside.

When, standing on the sidewalk, she thanked him for a pleasant weekend, he took her proffered hand and said, 'The pleasure was all mine.'

Then, before she could guess his intention, he stooped and kissed her lightly on the cheek. 'Goodnight, Sera. Sleep well.'

A moment later the silver-grey limousine was drawing away.

It seemed as though she'd misread his intentions after all, she thought as she climbed the stairs. His behaviour throughout the weekend had been that of a genial host. Nothing more. Nothing less.

Admittedly he'd kissed her cheek, but it had been a mere peck, and he'd kissed his other female guests in exactly the same way...

The light on the top of the landing was dim and, head down and fumbling in her bag for her key, she had almost reached her door before she noticed the figure leaning against it.

Straightening up, Keir demanded, 'Where on earth have you been? I was becoming seriously concerned.'

Sera gave a gasp and her nerveless fingers dropped the key.

Stooping to pick it up, Keir unlocked the door and, when she went inside, followed her.

'I didn't think you were home,' she said weakly. 'There was no light on.'

'Oh, yes, I was home.' Though he didn't raise his voice, she could see by the white line around his mouth that he was controlling his anger only with an effort.

Feeling a sudden wild hope that she might have been mistaken about Cheryl, Sera asked, 'Have you been home all weekend?'

'No, I've been away on business.'

'Where?'

'The Catskills.'

So she hadn't been mistaken. And how *could* he be deceitful enough to call it business?

Watching her drop her weekend case on the bed, his dark blue eyes as cold as the Arctic Ocean, Keir pointed out tersely, 'You haven't answered my question. Where have you been? And, before you decide to lie, let me mention that I just saw you getting out of Rothwell's car.'

'*I've* no intention of lying,' she cried furiously. 'But where I've been has absolutely nothing to do with you.'

Taking her shoulders, he demanded, 'Tell me, Sera.'

'Very well.' She lifted her chin. 'I've spent the weekend at Martin's house on Long Island.'

His white teeth snapped together. 'Do you know what kind of reputation Rothwell has where women are concerned?'

'I don't care what kind of reputation he has.'

Keir's fingers tightened and he shook her a little. 'Sera, don't be a fool. He's a dangerous man. You're a damn sight too young and innocent to—'

Twisting free, she pointed out jerkily, 'I might be young, but I'm no longer quite so innocent,' and watched a dark flush appear along his hard cheekbones.

'In any case,' she went on hardily, 'there were ten other guests present and Martin behaved like a perfect gentleman.'

'I saw him kiss you.'

'He kissed all his female guests like that.'

With dangerous quietness, Keir enquired, 'And did he *buy clothes* for them all? Or are you going to try and tell me you can suddenly afford designer labels?'

'No, I can't afford designer labels.'

'So what did you have to do to earn that little number?'

Her hand swung up and gave his tanned cheek a stinging slap.

He caught her wrist and said trenchantly, 'Don't ever do that again.'

'Then, don't insult me. If I *had* decided to sleep with him I wouldn't expect to be paid for it.'

'*Have* you slept with him, Sera?' Keir demanded. Then urgently he said, 'For God's sake tell me you haven't.'

'Have you slept with Cheryl?'

Curtly, he said, 'I don't see what that has to do with it.'

The old double standards, she thought bitterly. 'And I don't see what business it is of yours who I've slept with.'

He took both her hands in his and urged, 'Please, Sera, listen to me. I thought we had an understanding—'

Breaking off abruptly, he took a sharp breath. 'I see you've decided not to risk it.'

Too agitated to realize what he meant, she asked, 'Risk what?'

'Your finger turning green. They say Rothwell's not ungenerous so, if you play your cards right, you should be able to get a diamond as big as a brick out of him.'

Dropping her hands, he swung on his heel. A second later the latch clicked quietly, but decisively, behind him.

Feeling sick and empty, Sera stood quite still, staring blindly at the chipped brown paint on the door. Would the outcome have been any different if she had still been wearing Keir's ring?

But how could it? The fact that she wasn't wearing it had made no difference to the way he'd spent his weekend.

How could he be so hypocritical, have such double standards? Did he really expect her to sit quietly at home waiting for him while he took another woman to the Catskills, and then swore it was business?

But the thing that hurt the most was the way he'd tried to cover his own misdeeds by putting her in the wrong. It confirmed all her previous doubts. He obviously cared nothing for her. All the feeling had been on her side.

Sad and sorry, angry and bitter by turns, the silk suit tossed in a careless heap on the chair, she lay awake going over the whole sorry mess until the early hours of the morning.

The instant she awoke, the previous night's quarrel filled her mind. But somehow, while she'd slept, her attitude had changed.

Recalling Keir's 'I was becoming seriously concerned', she knew she had misjudged him. He might not love her, but she'd been wrong to think he cared nothing, and his anger and concern over her association with Martin had almost certainly been genuine.

So, if he wasn't serious about Cheryl, and if she explained about the suit and her reason for accepting Martin's invitation, there might still be a chance to put things right.

She knew with complete and utter certainty that Keir was the only man for her, the only man she would ever give her heart and soul to. If he needed a woman, she would happily live with him without making any demands or expecting any commitments.

Maybe all she had to do was tell him.

A glance at her watch showed it had just turned half past six. Almost tumbling out of bed in her haste, she pulled on her dressing gown and went to knock on his door.

There was no answer.

It was a fine, sunny morning. He might be out jogging.

Going back to her own room, she showered and dressed as quickly as possible before hurrying downstairs and into the cool leafiness of the nearby park where they had often walked together.

At a brisk trot, she followed the route they usually took, but starting from the opposite end in case he should be coming back.

A young couple strolled slowly along, holding hands, followed by an elderly man walking a small black dog. Two youths, one with a canvas holdall slung from his shoulder, manoeuvred skateboards, while an old lady with white hair and a wrinkled face sat on a bench and fed the pigeons from a paper bag...

Sera sighed. There was no lack of people, but no glimpse of the man she sought so eagerly.

She was returning dejectedly to the Brownstone when she saw him coming out of the door. Her heart starting to pound, she quickened her pace.

As Keir reached the bottom of the steps a low-slung white sports car drew up at the kerb and the woman at the wheel, her hair a red-gold cap, leaned to wave through the open window.

He lifted his hand in answer and, saying something Sera

was too far away to catch, jumped into the front passenger seat.

A few seconds later the sleek car drew smoothly away and disappeared down the street.

Looking after it, feeling an almost unbearable anguish, Sera found herself wondering how anyone could survive such pain.

Having stood for a few minutes still and silent, she made a great effort to pull herself together. She should be thankful that somehow she had missed Keir.

If she'd found him earlier, she would have made a complete fool of herself. Now, though her heart felt as though it was broken, her pride was still intact.

And pride was all she had left.

When Sera arrived at the office, neatly dressed and with her head held high, there was no sign of her boss. But then, she had never expected Cheryl to be in.

The redhead had a reputation for working hard and playing even harder. It was clear that, at the moment, playing was paramount.

Sera had been at her desk for some half an hour when the phone shrilled.

'Hi!' Cheryl said. 'I wasn't planning to come in today. I know there's a lot to do, but can you hold the fort?'

'Yes, of course,' Sera's voice was as steady as she could make it. 'Are you ready for the Jaimeson deal to go through?'

'Yes. But hold back on the Dolland Park. I want them to sweat a little. If there's anything *really* urgent crops up that you feel you can't deal with, you can get me on the mobile. Otherwise I'll see you tomorrow.' She giggled suddenly. 'Or the day after if things really hot up.'

Replacing the receiver, Sera had a sudden, disturbingly

vivid picture of Cheryl and Keir in bed, their long legs tangled together, that bright head against his broad chest, and those red-tipped fingers running through his crisp, dark body hair.

Somehow she fought down her nausea and went back to work, concentrating with a kind of fierce desperation that carried her through the morning.

At lunch-time, Glenda, one of the secretaries from the main office, popped in with a packet of sandwiches and a coffee. 'Knowing you're on your own, I thought you could probably use these.'

'Thanks, that's kind of you.' Sera managed a smile.

The coffee was very welcome, but the sandwiches remained uneaten.

It was after six and most of the staff had gone when the office door opened and Martin walked in.

She looked up, startled. As far as she was aware, Martin never came into this office. It was always Cheryl who went to see him.

'I'm afraid Miss Rothwell isn't here,' Sera said.

'I know. I wouldn't be here myself, only my PA went home sick, so I have an extra workload.'

His voice casual, he remarked, 'I understand Cheryl has gone off somewhere with Sutherlands?'

When Sera said nothing, his pale blue eyes on her face, he pursued, 'Do I take it she's stolen him from you?'

Sera lifted her chin. 'He wasn't mine in the first place.' Levelly, she added, 'And no woman can steal a man who isn't willing to go.'

'Bravo!' he applauded. 'I admire your spirit.' Then briskly he asked, 'Were you planning on staying much longer?'

'No...'

She hadn't actually planned to stay. It was just that there was nothing to go home for. Nothing there but loneliness.

'I was intending to go as soon as I've finished this analysis.'

'Leave it,' he instructed. 'Glenda told me you'd worked right through lunch, so you've done plenty for one day. Come and have a meal. There's just enough time. Then I've got tickets for that show you wanted to see.'

'But I'm not dressed for going out,' she protested.

'You look fine to me. Come on.' Martin was a determined man who never took no for an answer when it was something he wanted.

Weary, her spirits at their lowest ebb, Sera put up no resistance when, gathering up her light jacket and handbag, he fairly hustled her out of the office and into the elevator.

The following day, saying his own PA looked as if she would be off for a while, Martin had borrowed her from Cheryl.

Sera had gone willingly, preferring, in the circumstances, to work for him rather than his sister.

That accomplished, Martin had leashed his impatience. He knew that with so much at stake this was no time to rush things. It would pay him to move slowly, to play a waiting game rather than scare her off.

During working hours, therefore, Sera found he was the perfect boss—friendly in a businesslike way, good-tempered, patient, always considerate.

To her relief she saw hardly anything of Cheryl and, when Martin's own PA failed to return, Sera accepted the post on a permanent basis.

Out of working hours Martin was good company, easy to talk to and fun to be with. He never attempted to touch her or kiss her, but treated her like a cherished younger sister.

She found herself being taken charge of, looked after, almost cosseted. She mattered. It was balm to her wounded soul.

Unlike herself, he'd been brought up to be sociable and enjoyed having people around him. Brushing aside her quibbles about clothes—and careful not to suggest buying her any—he took her to shows and concerts, to nightclubs and expensive restaurants, and to join the weekend house parties he was so fond of giving.

Truly grateful, she almost managed to convince herself that she was enjoying it all.

Keir's name was never mentioned and Sera saw nothing of him until one day, when she was about to get into Martin's car, she looked up and noticed him standing on the sidewalk watching her.

As she hesitated, he turned his back and walked away.

The following week it was Martin's birthday and, when they'd seen a show, they went on to Sky Windows to celebrate.

After an excellent meal, during which Sera drank a great deal more champagne than she was used to, he took her hand and, raising it to his lips, said with great seriousness, 'I love you, Sera. I've loved you from the first moment I saw you. Will you marry me?'

It was a sweet, romantic proposal, filled with warmth and genuine affection. She hesitated.

'If you'll only say yes, you'll make me the happiest man in the world,' he urged, 'and I'll spend the rest of my life making you happy.'

'Yes, I'll marry you.' As though he'd willed her, the words were out. Her promise given.

His expression taut, as if he was struggling to hold back

an excitement almost too great to be borne, he felt in his pocket and, producing a small leather box, flicked open the lid.

A moment later he slipped a dazzling half hoop of diamonds onto her finger and said, 'Feel free to change it if you'd prefer something different.'

Looking down at it, she thought of the cheap silver ring Keir had bought her, and wanted to cry.

Instead she smiled brilliantly and said, 'It's beautiful.'

Perhaps even then, in her heart of hearts, she knew she should never have accepted it...

A sudden whiz, as a figure brushed past too close for comfort, jolted Sera out of her abstraction. Coming back from the past abruptly into the early morning quiet of Central Park, she turned to see a youth on skates, a pile of newspapers folded under one arm, disappearing into the distance.

By her side, Keir said shortly, 'Careless young fool. Did he bump you?'

'No, he just startled me.'

Blinking and slightly dazed, like someone roused too suddenly from sleep, Sera realized they had reached the point where she usually left the Park.

Turning to her companion, she said with quiet finality, 'I have to go now.'

Taking off his sweat-band, Keir thrust it into his pocket and, running a hand through his black curly hair, cut shorter than she remembered, suggested evenly, 'Let me buy you a coffee. There's a breakfast bar just round the corner that opens at six.'

Part of her, that old treacherous part that still loved him, urged her to accept. But she knew that, for a number of reasons, it was far too dangerous.

For one thing, if Martin had had a bad night he might wake early and ask for her and, if she wasn't there, it would cause the kind of problems she didn't want to have to face.

And that was putting it mildly.

She shook her head. 'I ought to be getting back.'

A glint in his eye, Keir dispensed with the velvet glove. 'Perhaps I'd better lay it on the line. I've no intention of letting you go until we've had more chance to talk.'

The last thing she wanted to do was talk, but she knew of old that, in this mood, Keir was implacable.

Still suffering from shock and feeling unable to fight that steely determination, she gave in. 'Very well, but I won't have to be too long.'

CHAPTER FOUR

AS THOUGH uncertain whether to trust her sudden capitulation, Keir took her hand and, twining his fingers in hers, began to lead her in the opposite direction to the one she needed to go.

The Red Rooster coffee bar was already busy, the high stools around the counter half full of mainly track-suited customers.

Keir chose a small table by the window and ordered two cappuccinos, which arrived promptly, accompanied by a plate of sugary doughnuts.

Leaving the doughnuts untouched they drank in silence until, eyeing her over his cup, he asked levelly, 'Why look so worried?'

'They'll be expecting me back.'

'Who's *they*?'

'W-well, Martin,' she stammered.

The firm mouth tightened. 'So you live with him?'

'I live in the same apartment.'

'Does that mean you're holding out for a wedding ring before you sleep with him?'

'It means I live in the same apartment.'

'I can't see Cheryl playing chaperon.'

Sera swallowed. 'She moved out when she got married.'

'And she married Roberto Canelli.'

It was a statement rather than a question and, wondering how he knew, she said, 'Yes.'

'So how long have you been living there?'

After the accident she had remained in a coma for almost five weeks before regaining consciousness. Then, having to spend a long time convalescing in a private nursing home, she had been forced to give up her room.

When she was fit enough to leave the nursing home, Martin, who had insisted on being cared for at home, had urged her to move in with him.

'You can use Cheryl's suite; she doesn't need it any longer.'

Having nowhere else to go, she had reluctantly agreed…

'Or is it a state secret?' Keir pressed when she didn't immediately respond.

'About seven months,' she admitted, and thought that it seemed a great deal longer. A prison, however luxurious, is still a prison.

His heavy-lidded eyes, with their thick sooty lashes, narrowed and thoughtful, he remarked, 'You're out exercising very early. Are you by any chance still going into the office?'

As soon as she had recovered her strength, hating the feeling of being dependent on Martin, she had stated her intention of going back to work and finding an apartment to rent.

With severe spinal injuries, he'd still been very poorly and in a lot of pain. When he'd begged her not to leave him, at least for the time being, she had felt forced to stay.

Some time later, when she could see he was making good progress, she'd broached the subject again.

He'd vetoed the idea, saying that as neither he nor Cheryl were at the office, there was no job open for her and, as soon as he was fit enough, he'd be working from home and he'd need her there with him.

When, in desperation, she'd attempted to argue, he'd flown into a rage and accused her of wanting to abandon him now that he was crippled.

Unable to bear that kind of moral pressure, she'd given in…

She became aware that, watching her face, Keir was still waiting quietly for an answer.

When she said nothing, he raised a dark brow. 'Well, Sera?'

She shook her head and felt the hot colour flood into her face as she realized what conclusions he would draw from that.

'A free woman with no need to work and unlimited money to spend! You must be in seventh heaven.'

It was so far from the truth that it was almost laughable, she thought bitterly. And she wondered what he'd say if he knew the true situation.

'You seem to think I'm obsessed with money,' she objected.

'What else can I think? Though, after the kind of childhood you had, I suppose I shouldn't blame you if you were looking for a rich husband who could give you all the things you'd ever wanted.'

'But I wasn't looking for a rich husband.'

Obviously unconvinced, he said, 'I was fool enough to imagine you loved me until Rothwell came along and rattled the moneybags.'

'How rich Martin was had absolutely nothing to do with it.'

'Then, what was the criteria? He was better-looking? More intelligent? Kinder to children and animals?'

With careful understatement, she said, 'He found time for me, gave me some attention.'

'You mean he bought you clothes… Took you places… Spent money on you when I had none to spend.'

Shaking her head, she insisted, 'It was nothing to do with money. *Nothing!*'

Then, realizing she would never convince him, she said curtly, 'Oh, what's the use? There's no point in talking about it. It's all over and done with. Nothing can be changed.'

'I'm not so sure about that,' Keir said icily. 'Rothwell deliberately set out to take you away from me...'

That, at least, was true. With a ruthless determination she'd only afterwards appreciated, Martin had played on her loneliness, her growing belief that Keir didn't care. He'd used every trick in the book to take her away from his rival.

Sera fought back. 'But he would never have succeeded if you hadn't been involved with Cheryl.'

Keir seemed to freeze and, as a background to his silence, she heard the hum of talk, the hiss of the coffee machine, the rattle of cups and saucers...

Then, carefully, he said, 'I was never *involved* with Cheryl.'

Why was he still bothering to lie? she wondered, and said flatly, 'I saw you having lunch together.'

'Having lunch together isn't a hanging offence.' His dark blue eyes narrowed. 'And it only happened once. It was a business lunch at Rands, and Cheryl paid.'

'You were holding her hand.'

'We *shook* hands, which is somewhat different...' His smile sardonic, he added, 'I suppose you were there with Rothwell?'

'And a Mr and Mrs Kessler. It was a business lunch. Martin asked me to take Cheryl's place as she wasn't available.

'When he picked me up he thought I needed a smarter outfit. That's why Anglo American provided something more suitable.'

'Really?'

'Yes, really,' she said angrily.

'Wasn't it so you'd have something *more suitable* to wear for your weekend in Long Island?'

'At that time I didn't know I was going to be invited to go to Long Island.'

'I bet Rothwell did.'

'If you hadn't been taking Cheryl to the Catskills I wouldn't have gone.'

'I wasn't taking Cheryl to the Catskills.'

'Martin mentioned that she was going there to have a romantic away-from-it-all break with her latest man. And you admitted you'd been to the Catskills.'

Keir's lips tightened. 'So that's why you asked me if I'd slept with Cheryl...'

Then, with a sigh, he said, 'The fact that I'd been to the Catskills the same weekend, doesn't mean I was Cheryl's latest man. My trip was purely business. I told you so at the time.

'Roberto Canelli, who, incidentally *was* Cheryl's latest man, had a parcel of real estate up there he wanted me to handle.'

'Roberto?' Sera whispered.

'If you remember, Cheryl introduced me to him the night of the party. After we'd looked at the proposed re-location site for his business, we went back to his apartment to thrash out some details.

'About two-thirty in the morning I took a taxi home. Cheryl stayed there.'

'You came back that night?'

'Yes. There was still a chink of light under your door, but I decided not to disturb you.'

'I left the light on on purpose hoping you'd knock.'

'It was so late, I felt sure you'd be asleep...'

With a sigh, he admitted, 'And that wasn't the only

reason... The way I was feeling then, if I'd come in I would have stayed, and I didn't want to do that.'

Her voice barely above a whisper, she asked, 'Why not?'

'Because I couldn't treat you as though you were some casual affair. At that stage of the game I had nothing to offer you. No time. No money. No security. My whole future hung in the balance, and if things had gone wrong...' One long, well-shaped hand made a movement of finality.

Sera swallowed hard. 'I went to your door the next morning. You weren't at home.'

'I left for the office at six-thirty. There was a very full day ahead. Several hours of work to catch up on, then a business lunch with Cheryl and Canelli, followed by a trip to the Catskills.

'At the last minute Canelli phoned to say he couldn't make lunch, but the Catskill trip was still on and he'd pick us up on the corner of Madison and East 88th Street.

'Everything seemed to be going well until I got back on Sunday afternoon and found there was no sign of you. By the time you turned up I was almost out of my mind with worry.

'When I saw you get out of Rothwell's car...saw him kiss you...saw you wearing clothes I knew damn well you could never have afforded to buy yourself, I was furious... Then I found you'd taken off your ring...

'The following morning I came to your door to apologize for the way I'd treated you, but you weren't there. I couldn't hang about, Cheryl was picking me up for a breakfast meeting with Canelli...'

'I saw her,' Sera said through stiff lips, and wondered how life could be so cruel? When she'd knocked at Keir's door, he must have been in the shower, and when he'd knocked at hers, she'd been in the park looking for him.

She wanted to weep, to rail against a fate that had offered her happiness only to snatch it away again.

But how much was due to fate and how much to human intervention? It had been Martin who had dealt the *coup de grâce*.

She could see his face now, the calculating glance as he'd said, 'I understand Cheryl has gone off somewhere with Sutherlands? Do I take it she's stolen him from you?'

Sera knew that it had been no mistake on his part, he'd done it quite deliberately, and her reaction, she realized bitterly, must have been exactly what he'd hoped for.

If she'd had the guts to tackle Keir, ask him outright how things stood, she would no doubt have discovered the truth.

But the indisputable fact that he'd had no time for her had convinced her that he couldn't really care, and her pride had insisted that she walk away.

'I tried again that evening,' Keir went on after a minute, his voice level, 'but you were out with Rothwell. I saw him bring you back very late.

'That's when I realized how hopeless it was... At the time there was no way I could compete, and I couldn't really blame you for not being prepared to wait until I had money to—'

'I didn't want your money,' she broke in fiercely. 'The only thing I ever wanted from you was for you to sometimes be there for me. But you hardly ever were. Business always came first...'

It was that, more than anything, that was responsible for the break up. If he hadn't abandoned her that night at the party...

'It's true I neglected you,' he admitted heavily. 'But, unfortunately, I had little option.

'I was in my first year at Oxford when my mother died. It was sudden and totally unexpected, and my father, who had worshipped her, went completely to pieces and started to drink heavily.

'At that time the business was worth hundreds of millions but, overnight, he seemed to lose all interest, along with the will to live.

'He made so many mistakes and errors of judgement that, before I'd finished college and returned home, Sutherlands had started to go downhill.

'But it wasn't until he finally drank himself to death that I discovered just how bad things were. All that was left was a house mortgaged up to the hilt and a business on the verge of bankruptcy.

'Because the house was just a liability, I got rid of it and took the cheapest apartment I could find Downtown. I needed to work all the hours God sent to have any chance of saving Sutherlands...'

Feeling as though a knife was turning in her heart, Sera wondered why he hadn't told her all this at the time rather than telling her now, when it was much too late?

Bleakly, he added, 'I didn't mind until I met you...'

'If you'd only told me *why* you were working such long hours, I would have understood. But you never breathed a word about any difficulties.'

'I was trying to keep the whole thing under wraps. It's true to say that most property market deals, as well as financial ones, are based on confidence. Any hint of trouble and you're sunk.'

'But you could have told *me*.'

'In all fairness, I thought it best not to. After all, you

worked for Anglo American and you might have found yourself with divided loyalties.'

As she began to shake her head, he went on, 'You were aware that Rothwell had agreed to part-finance that big Broadway development...'

It was a statement rather than a question, but she answered, 'Yes.'

'I'd poured my few remaining resources into that project. It was a gamble, but I knew that if it came off it would be the first step towards putting Sutherlands back on top. I also knew that if Rothwell got wind of any difficulties he'd withdraw his offer, and that would be the end...'

Painfully, she said, 'I wish you'd had more faith in me. I wish you'd told me.'

'Would it have made any difference?'

'Yes, it would.'

All the difference in the world.

Knowing how things were, she would have understood and given him her full support, rather than presuming he didn't care about her. She would have been content to wait and, if things hadn't turned out right, she would have stuck by him if he hadn't had a penny.

But the knowledge had come too late. Now she was trapped and there was no way out.

A kind of shudder ran through her.

'Cold?' Keir queried.

'A little.' All the way through to her soul.

'You look pale and thin, as though you've lost weight,' he pursued. 'Have you been ill?'

'No.' She hadn't been ill in the way that he meant.

'Then, what's wrong?'

Suddenly they were on dangerous ground.

'Nothing's wrong,' she denied quickly. Jumping to her

feet, her voice strained, she added, 'I must be getting back.'

His fingers closed lightly round her wrist, not hurting, just keeping her there. 'Why the hurry? It's still quite early.'

Martin, as part of his daily routine, had breakfast before he got up and he liked her to sit on the bed and share it.

Without stopping to think, she spoke the truth. 'If Martin's awake he'll expect me to have breakfast with him.'

As though picking up her thought waves, Keir said, 'Breakfast in bed, no doubt? How very cosy.'

Watching the colour mount in her cheeks, he added caustically, 'In fact, it sounds for all the world like connubial bliss.''

Biting her lip, she begged, 'Please, Keir...'

He rose to his feet, dwarfing her five feet seven. 'Very well, I'll walk home with you.'

'I'd rather you didn't,' she protested hurriedly.

'Why not? If he's missed you, will he be waiting at the door rattling your chains?'

It was too close to the truth to be funny.

When she made no answer, he released her wrist, dropped some dollar bills on to the table and, his hand at her waist, accompanied her to the door.

By now the city was stretching and yawning, the street stirring into life ready to face a new day.

As they walked along the still almost deserted sidewalk, Sera was very aware of the man by her side. Aware also that her veneer of self-possession was dangerously thin, her defenses as brittle as glass armour.

His sudden reappearance in her life, the knowledge that he had loved her after all and only the most unkind circumstances had deprived them both of the happiness they might have had together, had hit her very hard.

Somehow she had to take a grip on the situation, to forestall any further awkward questions, and keep her defences intact until he left her.

With that in mind, she made an effort to steer the conversation into safer, if no less painful, channels. 'How long have you been back in New York?'

'For the last six weeks.'

It gave her a strange, hollow feeling to think that he had been right here on her doorstep, when she had imagined him so far away.

With a kind of wry self-mockery he added, 'While I've been gone I've missed the bright lights. Though I love England and I've spent a lot of time there, I've always regarded New York as home, and this best part of a year has seemed endless.'

Almost a year. So much could happen in a year.

For the first time it occurred to her that he might be in a steady relationship. He was a red-blooded male and, whether in England or the States, there would be no lack of eager females.

He'd only have to look at any woman he fancied with those fascinating eyes, smile that slow, slightly crooked smile...

He might even be *married*.

In all probability he was.

Without knowing quite why, she felt sure he was the marrying kind, and a man with his looks and charisma would have no difficulty finding a wife...

Though it seemed very dog in the manger, the thought gave her no pleasure.

'Are you married...or anything?' As soon as the question was out, she knew she shouldn't have asked. It betrayed too much. Angry with herself, she felt her colour rise.

'No, I'm not married. As for the rest...' he gave her a quizzical glance. '...I'm not quite sure what you mean by "or anything"?'

Her colour deepening, she gritted her teeth and said nothing.

'A live-in lover, perhaps?' he suggested.

When she remained silent, he queried, 'Would it bother you if I said I have?'

'It wouldn't bother me in the slightest,' she lied hardily. 'I don't care if you have a harem.'

'Hardly my style,' he answered lightly. 'Though I don't enjoy living like a monk, basically, as my father and my grandfather were before me, I'm a one-woman man.'

If only *she* could have been that woman.

Biting her lip, she backtracked to ask, 'Will you be in the States for much longer?'

'I'm home for good now that my grandfather's died.'

'Oh, I'm sorry.' She knew he had been very fond of the old man.

'His health had been failing for some time and he knew he had only a matter of months to live. That was the main reason I went over to England, to help him sort out his affairs.'

'How long has he been dead?'

'He died in December. I would have come home sooner, but I needed to find a first class man to run the UK business side of things.'

Gladness in her voice, she said, 'Speaking of business, I gather from the latest financial reports that Sutherlands is doing very well.'

'I bet Rothwell *is* pleased,' Keir remarked sarcastically.

Martin, looking anything but pleased by the news, had

failed to hide his chagrin but, unwilling to aggravate old enmities, Sera said steadily, 'Why shouldn't he be pleased?'

Keir laughed mirthlessly. 'Oh, come on! You know he's always hated my guts. It must really choke him to know I'm finally succeeding.'

'I think you're exaggerating.' Desperate to be fair, she added, 'After all, Martin did help to finance that big Broadway project that meant so much to you.'

His face set and hard, Keir observed icily, 'Why pretend? You know quite well that Rothwell withdrew his support.'

Then, seeing Sera's stricken expression, he asked, 'You *didn't* know?'

Dry-mouthed, she said, 'No, I didn't know.'

'He waited until the last possible minute,' Keir went on evenly, 'when he must have felt sure I'd find it impossible to get finance anywhere else.'

Sera had been well aware that there was no love lost between the two men, but she hadn't realized Martin could be so ruthless and vindictive.

With that unnerving way he had of echoing her thoughts, Keir said grimly, 'Oh, yes, he did his best to make certain I was finished. He *wanted* to see Sutherlands go down.'

Unwilling to believe it, she made a gesture of repudiation. 'Surely he—'

'It's no use trying to cover for him. When I taxed him with it, he admitted as much. In fact, he was so sure he'd succeeded that he openly gloated. Regrettably, I lost my temper and knocked him down.'

Sera recalled the time Martin had had a bruised jaw and had been in a foul mood for days but, when she'd asked him what had happened, he'd made the excuse that he'd caught himself on the edge of a door.

Slowly, she said, 'But he didn't. Succeed, I mean... Though, if things were as bad as you've just told me, how did Sutherlands manage to survive?'

'I have my grandfather to thank for that. As luck would have it, he'd just sold off part of his holdings and freed up a large amount of capital. He offered me the finance I needed. Now, with the help of the internet, business is booming on both sides of the pond.'

'I'm so *pleased*!' she spoke fiercely, sincerely.

His dark face sardonic, he remarked, 'Perhaps you should have stuck with me after all. With what I've inherited from my grandfather, it's on the cards that I now have considerably more money than Rothwell...'

As, aware of a strange note in his voice, she looked up at him, he added flatly, 'That being the case, I want you back.'

Her heart lurched wildly and she caught her breath. Did that mean he still cared about her?

As though she'd asked the question aloud, he answered, 'Despite being totally disillusioned, I can't get you out of my mind. You still haunt me... Call it an obsession if you will. Rothwell isn't the only one entitled to feel that way... And, as far as he's concerned, I have a fancy to even the score. He bought you. Now I'm in a position to make a higher bid.'

Surely this was some kind of cruel joke? Sera thought dazedly. Taking a deep breath, she said, 'You can't be serious!'

'I assure you I am. You don't love me, you may not even like me, but you once found money and power were an aphrodisiac, and now I have both. If you finish with Rothwell and come back to me, I've enough money to be able to buy you a diamond ring for every finger and provide whatever kind of lifestyle you fancy—in short, give you everything your heart desires.'

She bit her lip savagely. The irony, had he known it, was that he didn't need to have a penny to give her everything her heart desired. All she'd ever wanted was for him to love her.

And it was plain that he no longer did in spite of his declarations.

This was no lover's approach. It was hard, cynical, motivated by a desire for revenge. He might want her, but his main aim was undoubtedly to get even with the man who was his enemy and his rival.

When she was sure of her voice, she said, 'I'm afraid you're wasting your time. If you were as rich as Croesus it wouldn't make any difference. I'm not for sale to any man.'

'Don't try to tell me you actually *love* Rothwell?' he sneered.

'Very well, I won't.' At the end of her tether, she quickened her steps until she was almost running.

Keir kept pace effortlessly. 'I believe if you really loved him you would have married him by now.'

'Believe what you like!' she snapped.

'I'm curious to know why you're not already married. I can't imagine this long delay was Rothwell's idea. He was mad about you from the word go. He couldn't wait to marry you...'

For the first time ever it was a relief to Sera when she reached the Warburton Building—she could never think of it as home—and made her way to the side entrance.

She had pulled open the door and was about to hurry inside, when Keir's hand on her arm halted her.

'Aren't you at least going to say goodbye?'

Head down, she whispered, 'Goodbye.' The awful finality of it caught in her throat and stuck there.

His free hand slid beneath her chin and lifted her face to his. For a heart-stopping instant, blue eyes looked into green. Then he bent his dark head and kissed her.

She made a little sound, halfway between a sigh and a sob, while the world and everything in it ceased to exist. His mouth on hers, his arms holding her, were the only things that were real, the only things that mattered.

When he finally released her, dazed and disorientated, her eyes open but unseeing, she staggered.

He took her shoulders and steadied her.

For a brief moment, the pure joy of his kiss lingered, then the world and all its problems came rushing back to overwhelm her.

With a little, incoherent murmur, she turned blindly away.

Keir slipped an arm around her waist and began to walk across the still deserted foyer with her.

Lifting a head that felt too heavy for her slender neck, she asked thickly, 'What are you doing?'

Dark brows raised in mock surprise, he told her, 'Walking to the elevator with you.'

'No, you can't,' she protested.

With exaggerated patience, he said, 'Don't be silly. Of course I can.'

'Please don't,' she begged. 'Please just go.'

'Go where?'

'Home... Wherever you live.'

'This is where I live.'

Thinking she'd misheard him, Sera stopped and stared at him.

Dark blue eyes gleaming, he repeated, 'This is where I live.'

'It can't be.' Then, in bewilderment, she said, 'I don't understand.'

Patiently, he said, 'When I came back to New York I moved in here.'

'Moved in here?' she echoed blankly.

'Now, you've got it,' he said encouragingly.

'Then why did you kiss me goodbye?'

'Oh, I didn't kiss you *goodbye*. I just kissed you.'

She swallowed. 'And you really *do* live here?'

'I really do.'

Had he moved into the same building on purpose? Or was this some strange coincidence? No, surely not. It was stretching credibility too far to believe that, with all the accommodation available in New York, the move hadn't been carefully planned.

Unless the whole thing was merely some elaborate leg-pull?

'Which floor?' she demanded.

'I'm living directly above you in the Penthouse.'

'No, you can't be...'

She knew that couldn't be so, because when Martin had left the hospital he had wanted to move into the Penthouse, so he could have a roof garden. But when approached, the elderly tenant, a Mr Cyrus Cornell, had steadfastly refused to move out, despite being offered a very substantial 'inconvenience' payment.

'The penthouse is occupied by a Mr Cornell.'

'*Was* occupied by a Mr Cornell,' Keir corrected her. 'I particularly wanted the Penthouse,' he added. 'So when I discovered that Cornell, who's recently retired, was looking for a house near the sea, I pulled out all the stops to find him just what he wanted at West Hampton... So, you see, we're neighbours again.'

Speechless, Sera found herself escorted into the elevator.

They had it to themselves, but Keir seemed to fill the space with his height and his breadth and his sheer masculinity.

Finding her breath impeded, she moved as far away from him as the space would allow, and they rode up in silence while she struggled to make sense of what she'd just been told.

What was he up to? What did he hope to gain?

Remembering his 'I particularly wanted the Penthouse', she found herself wondering if this moving in a floor above his old rival was symbolic.

Then, more urgently, she wondered what Martin would say when he found out that Keir had succeeded in getting the Penthouse when he'd failed. No doubt he'd be absolutely furious...

When they came to a halt and the doors opened, her head full of confused thoughts, Sera stepped out and was halfway across the carpeted passage before she realized she was on the wrong floor.

As she attempted to turn back, the elevator doors slid shut.

Keir had unlocked the door to the Penthouse and, before she could catch her breath, he threw an arm around her waist and propelled her inside.

Her first impression was of lightness and space, and she soon realized why. The living-room was on the corner of the building, and almost the whole of the outer walls were made of glass.

Several of the panels, which led on to a paved terrace, had been left open, and the early morning air, redolent of sunshine and flowers, was filling the room.

'Come and have a look at the garden.'

'No. I—I can't stop. I really can't stop.'

But, when she turned to escape, Keir was leaning casually against the door, his broad shoulders against the white and gold panel.

'I need to get back,' she cried in a panic.

'What's the hurry? You don't have to go out to work. Let's have some more coffee. We can drink it on the terrace.'

'I can't wait for coffee.'

'It'll be ready,' he said imperturbably. 'I always leave the machine on for when I get back.'

As though to prove his words, the appetizing aroma of fresh coffee wafted in.

Shaking her head, she protested, 'But it's almost seven-thirty.'

'I'm sure Rothwell won't mind breakfasting alone for once.'

But he *would* mind. And if he knew who she was with, he'd go through the roof.

'Please, Keir...' Reduced to begging, she saw by his expression that he was enjoying holding the whip hand.

Shaking his head a little, he made a mocking gesture indicating that she should precede him.

Only too aware of how useless it was to resist, she made her way out on to the paved terrace, her steps leaden, her emotions in a turmoil.

CHAPTER FIVE

OUTSIDE, beneath a roofed area, there was a selection of practical-looking outdoor furniture, and a built-in bar with a coffee machine.

Encroaching a little onto the terrace was a garden bright with flowers and shrubs and, beyond the stone balustrade, a wonderful view over Central Park to Upper West Side.

Keir indicated a pair of loungers with a small glass-topped table between them and, sitting down reluctantly, she watched him pour two cups of coffee.

He handed her one and, as though making a point, sat down between her and the only escape route.

'Why are you doing this?' she cried in a sudden burst of anger. 'What is it you *want*?'

His smile wolfish, he said, 'You know quite well what I want, Sera.'

She put her untasted coffee down with a rattle. 'Revenge, presumably.'

'Revenge, certainly. But there's something I want a great deal more. You in my bed. It's been a long time. And, as I said before, I don't particularly enjoy living like a monk.'

'There are plenty of women.'

'It happens to be *you* I want.'

'I've already told you, I'm not for sale to any man.'

'Then, if money won't do the trick, I'll have to think of some other way to get you.'

'You're wasting your time,' she told him thickly.

81

Something about the way she spoke warned him that she meant it and, for an instant, he looked disconcerted.

Then a shutter came down, leaving his hard-boned face guarded, unreadable. With a slight shrug of those broad shoulders, he said, 'We'll see, shall we? In the meantime, suppose we finish our conversation?'

'As far as I'm concerned there's nothing more to be said.'

'Oh, but there's a great deal. For instance, there are a lot of things you've carefully avoided telling me, and I'd like to know why.'

A little breeze blew a stray tendril of black silky hair across her cheek and she tucked it behind her ear before saying warily, 'I don't know what you mean.'

'Earlier I asked why you and Rothwell weren't already married...' Watching her like a hawk, Keir hazarded, 'Could it be that he's in a wheelchair?'

For a second or two Sera remained frozen, before exclaiming jerkily, 'So you know!' Then, with a kind of helpless exasperation, she said, 'Why did you ask all those questions if you already knew how things were?'

'I wanted to hear *your* version.'

When she said nothing, he went on, 'Oddly enough, I hadn't heard about the accident until fairly recently. It came as something of a shock. I don't relish having to fight a man in a wheelchair...'

Watching her transparent face, he smiled grimly. 'And don't get the idea it's because I feel sorry for him.'

'Then, what...?'

'If you think about it, you'll see it gives him an almost insurmountable advantage.'

Though it seemed to turn all her ideas topsy-turvy, on reflection, she could see that Keir was right. Martin's condition was a weapon he'd already used to the full.

Biting her lip, she backtracked. 'But if you already knew everything, why—?'

'Ah, but I didn't. There's still quite a lot I don't know, and you seemed oddly reluctant to tell me anything…'

When she sat still and silent, he pursued, 'I understand it was a road accident?'

Faced with the prospect of talking about the thing that weighed so heavily on her mind, she lost colour and began to shiver.

Seeing that Keir was watching her intently, she made a great effort to pull herself together and her voice, as dispassionate as she could make it, answered, 'Yes, it was.'

'When did it happen?'

'Just after you left for England.'

'I hadn't appreciated it was quite that long ago,' he said slowly. 'So where did it happen? Tell me about it.'

'Long Island. We were on our way to Pine Cove to join one of Martin's weekend house parties—'

'In the limousine?'

'No, it was the chauffeur's weekend off.'

'Go on.'

'The car ran off the road on a bend and hit a tree…' Her voice faltered to a halt.

'No other vehicle was involved?'

'No.'

'Go on,' he urged once more.

'Both Martin and I were hurt.'

'How badly?'

'I had a fractured skull, a cracked collarbone and several broken ribs, one of which pierced a lung.'

Keir's skin seemed to tighten over his strong bones, making his face into a tanned mask. Almost curtly, he asked, 'What about Rothwell?'

She swallowed. 'Martin's injuries were a great deal worse. They were to his lower spine and pelvis…'

Seeing the look on Keir's face, she said quickly, 'No, it's not what you're thinking,' and heard his almost imperceptible sigh of relief.

'He's going to be all right in every way,' she went on determinedly. 'His doctors say that he should soon be almost fully recovered and on his feet again.'

'How soon?'

'They suggest late September.'

'And then he wants you to marry him?'

'Yes.'

'And will you?'

'Yes, I'll marry him,' she said steadily.

'Not if I can prevent it.'

'But you *can't*.' There was a kind of anguished finality in the words.

Keir's jaw tightened and, his dark blue eyes holding a look that seemed to pierce her very soul, he said, 'Tell me the truth, Sera… Do you really love Rothwell? If the answer's yes, I'll fade quietly away and never bother you again.'

For everyone's sake she struggled to frame the lie.

'The *truth*,' Keir insisted quietly.

'The truth is, as long as Martin still wants me, I can never leave him.'

A look of relief mingled with an almost savage satisfaction on his handsome face, Keir exclaimed jubilantly, 'Then, you *don't* love him! I couldn't believe you did, but I had to be sure.'

'I'm fond of him,' she said quietly. And, in an odd kind of way, it was true. Though he could be ruthless and vindictive, mean and tyrannical, he could also be kind and caring, generous and easygoing.

He had so many good points, so much about him that was likeable. If only he'd been more rational, not so *obsessed* with her, there might have been some way out of this mess. How many men really wanted a reluctant wife?

'I wouldn't have thought mere *fondness* was enough to make you marry him,' Keir remarked. 'And you keep assuring me it has nothing to do with money.'

'It hasn't.'

'Then, why do you stay with him?'

Wishing she'd kept silent and let him think it *was* to do with money, she bit her lip.

Watching her face, he hazarded, 'Is it because you feel trapped?'

Seeing clearly what he was getting at, she took a deep breath and said, with what conviction she could muster, 'Of course it isn't.'

It was a lie.

Almost from the moment she had let Martin slip the ring on her finger—or, at least, after the effects of too much champagne had worn off—Sera had had serious doubts.

But feeling she was committed, and unwilling to hurt him, she'd tried to tell herself that most brides-to-be must have some doubts, and had done her best to stifle them.

It was after Keir had gone back to England, and with the wedding only a couple of weeks away, that she faced the truth and admitted to herself that she had made a terrible mistake.

And with that knowledge was an affirmation of the simple fact that, though he might not want her, it was Keir she loved, and always would love.

For Martin she felt only gratitude and affection. Not enough for a lifetime together. If she went ahead and married him, with so little real feeling, she would be short-changing them both.

She had made several attempts to tell Martin how she felt, but he had refused to listen, saying any doubts she felt could be put down to pre-wedding nerves...

The weekend they were due to go to Pine Cove, however, she had set out with the firm intention of ending their engagement and giving him back his ring.

If she'd managed to do it *before* the accident, things might have been different. But she hadn't...

'I don't believe you,' Keir said calmly. 'I think you're marrying him because you feel you can't abandon him now he's crippled.'

'He's not crippled,' she flashed. 'At the worst, he'll have a slight limp.'

'Exactly. So why sacrifice yourself?'

He was getting much too close to the truth.

'What makes you think marrying a rich man will prove to be a sacrifice?'

The blue eyes glinted between their sooty lashes, 'So it comes down to money after all?'

'Isn't that what you've always thought?'

'Amongst other things. I once thought you loved me. Foolish of me, but there it is. I couldn't believe you'd give yourself to a man you didn't love... But perhaps it was simply sexual attraction?' Suddenly he was on his feet, bending over her, one hand on either arm of the lounger. 'Whatever it was, it's still there. I discovered that when I kissed you.'

As she began to shake her head in denial, his eyes on her mouth, he suggested, 'If you'd like me to prove it?'

'No, I wouldn't.' There was no mistaking her absolute panic. 'I'd like to go now. Please, Keir... It's getting late and Martin will be worried to death if he finds I'm missing.'

Straightening up, Keir asked slowly, 'Then, he doesn't know about these morning outings?'

'No,' she admitted.

'Why not?'

'I—I didn't think he'd approve.' Then, sharply, she said, 'You used the term "morning outings"... What makes you think this morning wasn't a one-off?'

Keir smiled crookedly. 'I often have a word with the night security guard... Bill, I think his name is... He takes quite a fatherly interest in you.'

'So when we bumped into each other, it wasn't just a chance meeting,' she said accusingly. 'You *knew* I went to the Park every morning, and you knew the route I took. You were lying in wait for me.'

'I'm not sure I like the term "lying in wait",' he objected mildly.

'Whether you like it or not, that's what you were doing,' she said hotly. 'How long have you been watching me?'

'Since I moved in here,' he admitted, adding, with more than a touch of self-derision, 'For quite a number of reasons, it took me a little while to unearth what I needed to know and work out my plan of campaign.'

In spite of the almost flippant way he spoke, Sera felt sure he was deadly serious.

But what could he do? He'd been the first to acknowledge that Martin had an almost insurmountable advantage, and if he'd known the full facts he would have omitted the word 'almost'...

Somewhere close at hand a clock began to chime the hour. Jumping to her feet, she cried in agitation, 'It's eight o'clock. I must go. Martin likes to start work by eight-thirty.'

'How long has he been able to work?'

'He began doing a little about four months ago.'

'Does he work most days?'

'Most mornings, for a few hours. Unless he's having a bad day.'

'And you work as his PA?'

'Yes.'

Sera answered Keir's questions because it seemed quicker, but she had a feeling that he already knew the answers and was simply ticking them off in some mental book.

'Then, I mustn't detain you any longer,' he said smoothly.

Hardly daring to believe he was letting her go, she hurried to the door. Though Keir only seemed to stroll, he reached it first and opened it for her.

As she hurried out without a backward glance, he said, 'See you in the Park tomorrow morning.'

The elevator didn't come immediately and, aware that he was standing in the doorway watching her, she made an effort to hide her agitation.

'As you're in such a hurry, it might be quicker to use the stairs,' he suggested.

Biting her lip, she followed his mocking advice and, after hurrying down one flight, let herself into Martin's air-conditioned apartment as quietly as possible.

If he'd slept late, as he occasionally did, he might not have missed her and if she could only get out of this track-suit and shower...

She was halfway across the hall when the living-room door slid open and Martin appeared in his wheelchair. He was already shaved and dressed and, with a sinking heart, she saw that his heavy face was livid with fear and anger.

With a sudden insight, she knew he'd been afraid that she might have gone for good.

'Where the hell have you been?' he demanded.

'Walking in the Park.' Only too aware that she'd sounded guilty, she added, 'I needed some exercise.'

'When you weren't in your room, I couldn't imagine where you'd got to. Why didn't you tell me you were going out?'

'I thought you'd be asleep.'

His pale eyes taking in her track suit and trainers, he said, 'This isn't the first time, is it?'

'No,' she admitted.

'How long have you been sneaking out like this?'

Flushing a little, she said, 'I've been going out on fine mornings for about seven or eight weeks.'

'If I'd known you intended to start exercising at the crack of dawn, I might have come with you. The fresh air would have done me good.'

She knew perfectly well that Martin had never cared either for fresh air or any form of exercise, apart from swimming.

He tended to be an indoors man, with a preference for cars and air-conditioning, and, if he hadn't expended so much energy when it came to business and socializing, he would have run to fat.

'Why don't you come in future?' she suggested evenly.

'A jogger and a man in a wheelchair? That should be good for a laugh!' he said savagely.

Wincing, she begged, 'Please, Martin, don't—'

He cut through her words ruthlessly. 'Until you've been confined like this, you can't begin to know what it's like.'

'But you'll soon be on your feet again.'

'And then I'll be able to go for a morning limp around the Park. That's really something to look forward to!'

'I wish you weren't so bitter,' she whispered.

'What else do you expect me to be when I'm tied here and you sneak off and leave me without a word?'

'I'm sorry, I—'

'But I'm damned if you'll go off and leave me again.' It was part bluster, part plea.

'No, I won't go again if you don't want me to,' she promised. Then, remembering Keir's, 'See you in the Park tomorrow morning', she felt a sudden, sharp regret.

It was followed almost instantly by relief. Now Martin had laid it on the line, she couldn't give way to the temptation to go...

'So there you are, back safe and sound.' Kathleen emerged from the living-room looking pretty and trim in her blue and white uniform. Her short curly hair was as black as Sera's, her eyes the colour of wet violets.

Above Martin's sandy-gold head the eyes of the two women met in perfect understanding.

'I told Himself he was getting in a tizzy over nothing,' she added in the soft Irish brogue that she often laid on for effect. 'But will he ever listen?'

Though only about the same age as Martin, Kathleen treated her charge as though he was a slightly unruly small boy, telling him off in no uncertain terms when he didn't follow his doctors' orders, ignoring his bursts of temper, soothing his fears and his pain with an almost maternal tenderness...

His first nurse, unable to cope, had left in tears after only a few days. The second had lasted a week before walking out.

Kathleen, with her quiet competence, her sunny nature and unfailing sense of humour, had proved to be a godsend.

When, in the early days, he'd been unable to sleep because of the pain and had wanted Sera, Kathleen had said firmly that Sera wasn't in a fit state to cope, and had packed the younger girl off to bed and sat up with him herself. She still did occasionally, when he had a problem or felt restless.

Though Martin complained that she was bossy, and grumbled when she beat him at cards or checkers, he'd come to rely on her, and Sera didn't dare contemplate the time when, her job finally done, Kathleen would leave.

'Now, I dare say you'll be wanting to shower and change and grab a bite of breakfast?' Kathleen suggested to Sera.

As Sera nodded, Kathleen turned to Martin. 'In that case, perhaps you can spare a little time to discuss the new therapy Dr Neilson suggested?'

'So long as it doesn't take too long,' he said grudgingly.

'I'll be as quick as I can,' Sera assured him. 'And I'm happy to skip breakfast if you're in a hurry to start work?'

'I won't be doing any work today.' His announcement surprised both the women. 'As soon as everyone's ready I'd like to set off for Pine Cove.'

'But I thought we weren't going until tomorrow?' Sera said.

'I've decided Kathleen was right...'

Widening her eyes, Kathleen exclaimed, 'Sure and bejabers, but aren't I always?'

Giving her a glance which was intended to be repressive but ended up tolerant, Martin went on, 'She suggested we should go to Pine Cove a day early. Her idea was to give me plenty of time to rest before the party, but it makes sense for another reason. On a Friday, at this time of year, when half of New York is trying to get out of town for the weekend, the traffic on the Long Island Expressway can be bumper to bumper.

'Bearing that in mind, I've asked Carlson to bring the car around for ten-thirty this morning.'

'If that's so,' Kathleen said crisply, 'then I've a million things to do.' With a touch of asperity, she added, 'Why is it men never make up their minds until the last minute?'

Martin's grin eased away the lines of pain from his face and made him look suddenly boyish. 'It's to keep women on their toes.'

'Huh!' Kathleen gave a mock indignant toss of her black curls.

His expression one of amusement, he went on, 'You're entitled to a night off, so make sure you pack something pretty for the party.'

'*If* I have time.'

'Women can always find time for things like that,' Martin said provokingly.

'Only when they're not looking after men.'

Satisfied she'd had the last word, Kathleen manoeuvred the wheelchair back into the living-room while Sera hurried off to shower and change.

As the hot water cascaded over her and steam misted the frosted glass of the shower cubicle, she tried not to think of Keir and of everything she had learnt that morning.

It was all in the past, over and done with. Even *he* couldn't change things. All she could hope was that, before Martin discovered he was back, Keir would realize how useless it was and go quietly away and leave them in peace.

In peace... How funny. How terribly funny. Her laugh was more like a sob.

Though what they had at the moment *was* peace compared to what it had been. Both Martin's sniping and his violent fits of rage had eased considerably of late and that, Sera knew quite well, was mainly because of Kathleen.

But if he found out that his old rival was back on the scene, even *she* might find it impossible to keep things on an even keel.

And there seemed little chance of his not finding out...

Despite the hot steamy air, Sera shivered. Common sense told her that any hope of Keir going quietly away was almost certainly a vain hope.

He wasn't the kind of man to give up without a struggle. As well as being a brilliant strategist, he was tough and determined. The bigger the odds against him, the harder he'd fight.

Only, though he didn't know it, circumstances had made these odds insurmountable.

If the accident had never happened...

But it had...

Towelling herself dry, Sera wondered yet again if this trip to Long Island was wise. Would it bring everything back too vividly?

As she'd lain unconscious she had no memory of the accident, but Martin had been trapped in the car, fully conscious and in terrible pain, for more than an hour.

It would be the first time they had travelled that stretch of road since the accident; the first time he had allowed friends and colleagues to see him in the wheelchair he detested so much.

But, please God, everything would work out...

'Think of it as a form of therapy,' Kathleen had said when Sera had mentioned her fears. 'Once he's been over the road where the accident took place, and once he's realized that being in a wheelchair doesn't make him any less of a man, we'll have routed a couple of bogeys, and be getting somewhere.'

Having great faith in Kathleen's experience, her calm, down-to-earth practicality, Sera had tried to stifle her fears. But now, completely thrown by the trauma of the morning, and with the trip about to get underway, they had returned in full force.

By the Saturday evening, realizing her fears had proved groundless, Sera gave thanks.

Earlier in the day there had been one or two tense moments when Martin's house guests had begun to arrive. But apparently pre-warned by Cheryl, no one had offered any undue sympathy or treated him in any way differently, so things had passed off without any harm being done.

Most of the guests were now here, apart from an old college friend who'd called to say he'd been delayed, and Cheryl and her husband who, with a cottage of their own in the Hamptons, were only coming for the actual party.

All in all it seemed to be working.

Sera had always considered Pine Cove to be too big and too grand, with its twenty-odd rooms and its marble-floored hall but, after spending months cooped up in the Fifth Avenue apartment, the house proved to be a nice change.

Kathleen, surprisingly, loved the place on sight.

Martin, having lived in virtual isolation for so long, was finding the company of other people pleasantly stimulating and, consequently, was looking younger and happier than he had done since the accident.

It was a lovely evening and, though the buffet had been set in the dining-room, the French windows leading to the terrace had been opened wide as they had in the adjoining living-room.

As well as the house guests, thirty or so friends and

neighbours had been invited and were arriving in small groups.

Looking relaxed and remarkably handsome in evening dress, Martin, with Sera by his side, received them, and soon the party was in full swing.

Kathleen, officially given the night off, had discarded her uniform for a purply-blue dress that almost exactly matched her eyes.

With a touch of make-up and sparkling amethyst drops in her neat lobes, she looked absolutely lovely, Sera thought, and found herself wondering why such an attractive young woman should give up virtually all her social life to be a nurse.

It must be a heart-warming vocation; something that was eminently satisfying in itself.

Having very little choice, Sera was wearing the ankle-length sheath in muted shades of green and dull silver that she'd bought for the Anglo American party.

Her silky black hair was taken up into a smooth, shining knot and, realizing how wan she looked, she'd applied her make-up with care.

Her only jewellery was the fine silver chain she habitually wore under her clothes, next to her skin. One loop lay snugly beneath the hollow at the base of her throat, the other longer loop disappeared into the bodice of her dress.

Earlier, as they were gathering on the terrace for pre-party drinks, sounding irritable, Martin had complained, 'I don't know why you didn't buy a new dress. It would be nice to see you wearing something decent for a change.'

Flushing a little, she'd bitten her tongue and said nothing. If she'd had even a small salary she might have bought a new dress rather than wear this one which provoked such painful memories. But as things were she couldn't bring herself to spend Martin's money.

To Kathleen, he'd remarked, 'You look absolutely stunning! I hadn't realized until now how beautiful your eyes are...'

Blushing rosily, for once in her life Kathleen had found nothing to say.

'Why don't you go and mingle a little?' he'd added. 'Enjoy the party. Sera will stay with me, so you can forget I exist.'

But now, watching Kathleen talking and laughing with the other guests, and obviously a big hit with the males present, Martin looked anything but pleased that she'd taken him at his word.

Concerned that it was going to spoil his evening, Sera never left his side for a moment and, dancing attendance on him, did her best to fill Kathleen's place as well as her own.

'Hi!' Cheryl, striking in gold lamé, her husband by her side, had appeared out of the throng.

Stooping to kiss her brother's cheek, she said, 'Sorry we're a bit late. I guess it's because we live too close. Isn't it always the way? So how are things going?'

'Very well,' Martin said without a great deal of conviction.

'Sera... How are you?' Roberto, short and stocky, fetchingly masculine, lifted her hand to his lips in a gesture that was as charming as it was unselfconscious.

With eyes so dark they looked almost black, a smile that lit up his whole face, and a fascinating accent, Cheryl's husband was one of the most attractive men she'd ever met, Sera thought. He was also one of the nicest.

While the two men shook hands, Cheryl gave her sister-in-law-to-be a quick hug, followed by a close scrutiny. 'You still seem a bit thin and pale.'

'I'm fine, really,' Sera said, adding, with perfect truth, 'You're looking fantastic.'

Cheryl, a shade plumper than she used to be, the hardness gone from her face, was fairly glowing with health and happiness. Marriage evidently suited her.

'That's what being in love does for you,' she said with a grin.

The men were talking and, drawing Sera a little to one side, she went on in an undertone, 'We're not planning to announce it yet, but I've got to tell someone or I'll burst with excitement... I'm going to have a baby!'

'I'm so pleased,' Sera said warmly. 'When is it due?'

'Not for seven months yet, but Roberto can't wait.' Her voice dropping even more, Cheryl confided, 'His first wife didn't want a family, that's why they eventually split up. He's so thrilled to be a prospective father that he'd shout it from the rooftops if I let him... But at the moment, all he's got is permission to tell Martin...'

Sighing blissfully, she added, 'I never thought it was possible to be this happy.'

Then, with a searching look, she said, 'I've noticed that, despite the good news about Martin, *you* don't look very happy.'

'Oh, I am,' Sera lied desperately. 'It was such a relief to know that he's going to be all right.'

'It should make it possible for you to have more freedom,' Cheryl said shrewdly. 'I did think Martin might loosen up a little when that Irish nurse of his proved to be such a blessing, but it seems as though—'

'I hope you two aren't planning to stand gossiping all evening?' Roberto asked.

'I've just been telling Sera our secret,' his wife informed him.

'Isn't it *wonderful*?' he beamed.

'Wonderful!' Sera assured him.

'Well, we'd better go and mingle,' Cheryl said. 'My dear brother isn't looking too pleased…'

Martin, a frown on his face, was staring at the little group.

'Talk to you later.'

'I wondered how much longer you were going to be,' Martin grumbled as she returned to his side.

'Cheryl was just telling me about the baby. Isn't it marvellous news?'

'That depends on whether or not you like children,' Martin observed drily. 'Personally, I can't raise much enthusiasm for cluttering up my life with squalling brats. To be honest I'd never imagined Cheryl wanting any either, though Roberto tells me they're both—' He stopped speaking abruptly.

Following his gaze, Sera caught her breath. Looking dangerously handsome in a well-cut evening jacket and black bow-tie, Keir was strolling towards them.

CHAPTER SIX

WHAT in heaven's name was Keir doing here? she wondered frantically. There was a gleam in his eye, an arrogant tilt to his dark head, that indicated trouble.

Was he just trying to stir things up a bit? Or was he intending to provoke some kind of showdown in front of everyone?

Almost immediately she dismissed the latter possibility. In his own way, Keir was self-contained, a rather private man. Certainly not one to wash dirty linen in public.

With an air of studied politeness, he inclined his head. 'Sera… Rothwell… I understand birthday wishes are in order?'

Sounding staggered, Martin said, 'I thought you were in England.'

'You also thought Sutherlands was finished. You were wrong on both counts.'

His fair face turning brick red, Martin demanded furiously, 'What the hell have you come here for? Nobody invited you.'

'Cheryl did as a matter of fact.'

'I don't believe it,' Martin blustered. 'She never said anything to me. And how did she know you were back?'

'We met in the elevator a few days ago when she was leaving your apartment.'

Sera made an involuntary movement and, as though afraid she was going to leave him, Martin caught her wrist.

'What were you doing in the Warburton Building?' he asked his tormentor sharply.

'I live there,' Keir answered calmly. 'In the Penthouse.' As he spoke he glanced at Sera with a little smile in his blue eyes.

Correctly interpreting that look, Martin's nostrils flared and his fingers tightened on Sera's wrist threatening to crush the delicate bones. 'You *knew* he lived there.'

'Yes,' she admitted, 'but not until—'

'We happened to meet in the Park,' Keir broke in smoothly, 'and I took her up to look over the place.'

'So that's why you've been sneaking off every morning, pretending to be jogging. You've been meeting him!'

'I've been doing no such thing,' Sera denied. 'I didn't even know Keir was back in New York until Thursday morning when I—'

'You lying little…!' Pulling himself up, he bit off the rest. 'I suppose *you* wanted him here?'

'No, I didn't. I had no idea he was coming.'

'Then, what made Cheryl invite him?'

'I don't know.' At the end of her tether, Sera put her free hand to her throbbing head.

'Are you all right?' Keir asked sharply.

'Just a headache,' she said through stiff lips.

'If it wasn't Sera's doing, why the devil did Cheryl invite you?' Martin demanded of the other man.

'Why shouldn't she?' Keir said coolly. '*We've* never had any quarrel.'

'She must know you're not welcome here.'

'Why? Have you told her that at our last meeting I knocked you down…? No, I didn't think you had. It's not the kind of thing you'd want to brag about.'

'Damn you, Sutherlands! I suppose you'd like to do it again?'

'If you were on your feet I'd be pleased to. As it is, you have the advantage of me.'

'Get out! Go on, get out, or I'll have you thrown out.'

Keir raised a dark, mocking brow. 'Dear me, what would everyone think if they knew you were threatening to throw out an officially invited guest without even offering him a drink?'

Throughout the exchange, Keir had kept his voice low but, getting steadily more irate, Martin was in danger of being overheard.

Sera, desperate to smooth things over, begged, 'Please, Martin, the party's going so well, don't make a scene in front of everyone and spoil things...'

'Well *you* get rid of him, then.'

Turning to Keir, she begged, 'Please, go, for my sake.'

The words were more revealing than she realized and Keir frowned. 'Don't worry,' he said quietly, 'I wasn't planning to be here long, but I'd like a word with you in private before I leave.'

'Sera stays here with me.'

'Surely that's up to her.'

'She stays with me.'

With an expression of cold contempt, Keir looked pointedly at the hand gripping Sera's wrist. 'She doesn't seem to have much option.'

After a long pause, Martin released his hold, leaving a livid white mark where his fingers had bitten in. Indicating that she was free, he said, 'Now ask her if she wants to go with you.'

His dark blue eyes fixed on Sera's pale face, Keir queried, 'Well, Sera?'

Standing quite still where she was, feeling like death, she shook her head mutely.

With undisguised triumph, Martin taunted, 'See? Why don't you get it into your thick head that you're wasting your time? Sera's mine...'

Keir's face went white under his tan, the skin stretched taut over the strong bone-structure.

'She'll do whatever I want her to do.' Martin rubbed it in.

'Well, hello…' Kathleen, suddenly appearing from nowhere, smiled at Keir. 'I didn't expect to see you here.'

If she had any idea how tense the situation was, she gave no sign.

Recovering streets ahead of the other two, Keir returned her smile and said, 'Cheryl invited me.'

'Oh…' Kathleen looked a bit confused. 'I didn't realize you knew each other, with you being fresh to New York…'

'Though I've only been back a matter of weeks, I've lived here before and done business with her husband, so you could say we're old friends.' Casually he added, 'Do you happen to know where she is? I haven't had a chance to say hello to her and Roberto yet.'

'I was talking to them only a minute ago, so come with me and I'll take you to them.'

With a smile at the other two, she turned and led Keir away.

Sera watched them go with a hollow feeling of reprieve, while Martin stared after them in helpless fury.

As far as she could judge by his expression, rather than anything else, it was the sight of Kathleen, her earrings sparkling, turning her head to smile up at his rival, that provoked such fierce anger.

'Damn the pair of them!' he exploded. Then, sharply, he asked, 'How does Kathleen come to know him?'

'I haven't the faintest idea,' Sera said shakily.

But whether they'd met by chance, or whether Keir had somehow arranged it, it was obvious now where he'd gleaned his information. On discovering that he knew the

Rothwells, just for an instant, Kathleen had looked disconcerted, as though wondering if she might possibly have been indiscreet.

Sera sighed deeply. The evening, which had seemed to be going so well, had turned into something of a nightmare for them all.

And the following days, she guessed, would be even worse. His temper uncertain at the best of times, Martin would be impossible to live with. Half convinced, despite her protestations, that she'd been meeting Keir behind his back, he would seize every opportunity to make her life a misery.

In the past, with tact and unspoken sympathy, Kathleen had managed to ease some of the burden, but if she too had innocently incurred his wrath, it boded ill for them both.

'I need to get out of here.' Martin's voice broke into Sera's anxious thoughts.

Pulling herself together, she asked, 'Would you like to go into the garden?'

'No, I want to get away from people. Make it the study.'

Because there were no elevators at Pine Cove, he was using a suite of rooms on the ground floor that the previous owner, a semi-invalid, had had converted for his own use and that of his nurse.

There were two bedrooms, each with its own bathroom, a sitting-room and a study. The study overlooked the small, sandy cove with a single pine tree that gave the house its name.

Turning away from the groups of laughing, talking guests, Sera wheeled the chair through the quiet part of the house to Martin's suite.

In the study, the French doors that led onto the rear terrace were open wide. It was a lovely summer evening with a warm breeze carrying the scent of sea, sand and flowers.

'Would you prefer to be outside or in?' she asked.

'I don't care,' he answered curtly, his mind clearly on other things.

Sera pushed the chair onto the terrace and, sitting down beside him in one of the garden chairs, waited for the inevitable questions and accusations.

They weren't long in coming.

'Why didn't you tell me Sutherlands was back?'

'I didn't want to spoil the weekend.' That had certainly been one of the reasons.

Martin began to gnaw at his thumbnail, a habit he had when he was angry or disturbed, before asking, 'How did you know he was back?'

'As he told you, I met him in the Park.'

'How many times have you met him? And I want the truth.'

'Only once. The day before yesterday. It was a chance meeting...' That was only half true. It hadn't been chance on Keir's part.

'If you hadn't got careless and come back so late I would never have known. You would have been able to go on deceiving me.'

About to say she hadn't been deceiving him, she bit her lip. By hiding those early morning outings, she'd been doing just that.

'How many times have you been up to his apartment?'

'Just the once. I didn't *mean* to go up then, only...'

While she tried to explain the circumstances, he looked at her with eyes as cold and pale as a glacier until she faltered to a halt.

'What were you doing up there to make you late back?'

'Just talking.'

'Did he tell you how he came to be living in the Penthouse?'

That obviously rankled, as she'd known it would.

'Mr Cornell was retiring,' she said carefully. 'He was looking for a house by the sea—'

'And I suppose Sutherlands found him one?'

'Yes.'

'What else did you talk about?'

'He told me he'd never been involved with Cheryl.'

'And you believed him?'

'Yes.' Her clear green eyes accusing, Sera went on, 'I know now it was Roberto who took her to the Catskills, and it was Roberto she was with when you tried to make me believe she was with Keir.'

'Sutherlands was at the Catskills.'

'On business.'

'My word, he *has* brainwashed you.'

'I can always go and ask Cheryl.' Sera made as if to rise.

'Wait!' Martin said sharply. 'Suppose he was there on business? Don't forget he had no time for you. Work was a lot more important.'

'And I'm sure you know why.'

He shrugged his heavy shoulders. 'So Sutherlands was in a mess.'

'How did you find out?'

'Cheryl, who at that stage fancied him, was curious as to why someone in his position should be living in some seedy downtown apartment block. I did some digging. I don't know what it is about men like that... But when I told her the score she was fool enough to try and help him.'

'Whereas you did the precise opposite.'

His expression wary, he looked at her from beneath almost colourless lashes. 'What do you mean exactly?'

'You withdrew from the Broadway project.'

'How could I do any other? The risk was too great.'

'Is that the only reason you did it?'

'Of course.'

The assurance rang false.

'You must have known the score for a little while. Why did you wait until the last minute to tell him you were pulling out? Wasn't it because you wanted to see Sutherlands go under?'

'I suppose *he* told you that?'

'It's the truth, isn't it?' Her green eyes flashed. 'And isn't it also the truth that it was when you crowed about it that he lost his temper and knocked you down?'

'All right,' Martin said angrily, 'so I hate his guts.'

'And you were jealous of him.'

'You know how I feel about you,' Martin said with barely suppressed violence. 'I felt that way from the start. I couldn't stand to see you look at him as though he was Mr Wonderful. I was as much of a man as he was and I could give you a damn sight more than he could... I still can. As soon as I get the OK from the doctors we'll be married...' When she said nothing, he added, 'You promised to marry me, and you owe me that much.'

When she remained silent, apparently scared by her lack of response, he seized her hand in a painful grip and said urgently, 'Just because he's back you won't change your mind? You won't leave me?'

Keir's coming back had altered nothing.

'I won't leave you while you need me,' she promised quietly.

Martin released her hand with a sigh.

'So this is where you're hiding.' Kathleen came along

the terrace, her high heels clicking on the paving, and smiled at her patient. 'Is everything all right? You look a bit het up.'

'I'm surprised you've found time to ask,' Martin remarked testily. 'I thought you were more interested in Sutherlands.'

Treating his small-boy tantrum with the contempt it deserved, she said in her put-on brogue, 'Well, now, he's a fine-looking man, so he is.'

Ignoring Martin's seething glance, she added with a sigh, 'Sure and begorra, those eyes could tempt any girl to throw her bonnet over the windmill.'

'If he's so fascinating I wonder you could bring yourself to leave him,' Martin burst out angrily.

'He's gone,' she announced regretfully, 'and without even a drink, because he's driving. He sent his apologies that he had to leave so soon, but said he felt sure you wouldn't mind *too* much.'

Showing his teeth in a smile that was more like a snarl, Martin muttered, 'I suppose that's his sense of humour.'

'Now, I like a man with a sense of humour,' Kathleen said serenely. 'Especially one who's willing to laugh at himself. In my opinion a lot of men sit and glower and take themselves far too seriously...'

Martin shot her a suspicious glance as though wondering if she was getting at him.

'Are you ready to go back and mingle?' she queried. 'After all it *is* your party, and several people have already asked where you are.'

'Before I go back, perhaps you might be good enough to tell me how you come to know Sutherlands?' he asked curtly.

'I might that,' she agreed. Then, turning to Sera, she said, 'Oh, by the way, Cheryl wanted a word. She was with a small group by the sunken garden.' Then, with a touch of concern, she said, 'You look terribly pale; are you feeling all right?'

Sera managed a smile. 'Yes, it's just a headache.'

'Well, if you'd like to go ahead, I'll sit and tell Himself what he wants to know... Before we miss too much of the party,' she added pointedly.

Martin scowled. 'You sound as if I'm nothing but a nuisance.'

'No more so than any man,' she assured him cheerfully, dropping into the chair Sera had just vacated.

Then, tongue-in-cheek, she said, 'And at least you have two things going for you... You're good-looking, and you pay me a salary.'

'I could always stop,' he threatened.

'Now, would you be wanting me to...?'

It sounded as if the pair were about to indulge in one of the frequent sparring matches they both seemed to enjoy, Sera thought, as she made her escape. Clever Kathleen. It was probably just what she needed to restore Martin's good humour.

Needing a minute or two to herself, Sera took the path that meandered along the side of the house before crossing to the stone balustrade to look over the sunken garden.

Apart from a young couple strolling along holding hands, there wasn't a soul in sight.

Though she felt in no mood for a party, she turned dutifully to head back towards the sound of music and laughter that were drifting across the lawn.

As she drew level with the tall, wrought-iron gate leading onto the sandy lane that ran down to the shore, it opened and Keir appeared.

Startled, she gasped, 'What are you doing back?'

'I haven't gone yet. I was waiting for you.'

Wondering how he knew she would be coming that way, she shook her head. 'Cheryl wants me.'

'I asked Kathleen to say that.'

'Why?' Sera demanded.

'Because I want to talk to you.'

'Please, Keir, Martin might see us.'

'Afraid of him?'

'No.'

It was the truth. She wasn't *afraid* of Martin. In an odd sort of way, she was more afraid of Keir.

Martin, with his cockiness and his temper tantrums, was like a small boy who, though he needed constant placating, was no real threat.

Whereas Keir was tough and dangerous, a formidable man who could make her tremble by merely looking at her.

'I just don't want him upset any further,' she burst out raggedly.

'In that case may I suggest a stroll down the lane to the beach? You can't see the lane from the ground floor of the house, the wall is too high, so that will prevent any of the partygoers seeing us together.'

'But there's nothing left to say.'

'I'm afraid I must disagree.'

He indicated a nearby bench. 'Or perhaps you'd prefer to sit here and talk?'

The bench was in full view of the house. If they sat there and Martin came on to the terrace... She shook her head.

'Then, a stroll it is.'

There was an air of quiet purpose about him that told her he intended to have his way, and all the while they stood here arguing there was always the risk of them being seen.

'Very well,' she agreed reluctantly. 'But I can't be long.' If Martin missed her it would only cause more trouble.

She turned and hurried through the gate.

Close on her heels, Keir pulled it shut behind them and latched it.

A white Mercedes was parked a few feet down the lane, its nose pointing towards the road, its front passenger door standing open.

As they passed, Sera glanced at it curiously, wondering why a guest should choose to leave his car there rather than on the gravelled apron where the rest were parked.

Of course it might not belong to a guest, it might be someone who...

The thought was never finished.

Half pushed, half lifted, she was bundled into the front passenger seat and the door slammed behind her.

Before she could gather her scattered wits, Keir was sliding behind the wheel.

'What are you doing?' she demanded.

'I thought we'd go for a drive instead.'

'I don't want to go for a drive!' She tried to open her door but the handle stubbornly refused to budge.

'I'm afraid you're wasting your time, I've adjusted it,' he told her coolly as he switched on the ignition and fastened his seat belt.

'Open it this minute,' she cried. 'I've no intention of going anywhere with you.'

He reached over but, instead of opening the door, he clicked the buckle of her seat belt into place and, a moment later, they were driving up the lane.

His admission that he'd tampered with the door handle made her realize that this was no spur of the moment decision to take a drive, but something he'd *planned* with great care.

Her heart began to race with suffocating speed.

When they reached the main highway Keir swung right and, after a series of traffic lights, turned onto quieter roads.

Making an effort to fight down her panic, she said as steadily as possible, 'I don't know what you think you're going to achieve by this.'

'Some time alone with you, at the very least. A chance to talk to you, to thrash things out.'

'How long will it take? I mustn't be very long.'

'How long it takes is up to you.'

Presumably by that he meant how willing she was to answer his questions. Partly reassured, she said, 'So this *is* just a drive and straight back?'

'Not exactly.'

Her heart in her mouth, she demanded, 'Then, what exactly is it?'

'Call it giving you time to come to your senses.'

'I prefer to call it abduction.'

'Let's not be melodramatic,' he said sardonically.

'The police will call it that.'

'And who'll be calling the police?'

'Martin.'

'I doubt it.'

'If I just vanish, he'll be frantic! Oh, please, Keir, don't do this. You're making things so much worse... I don't want him stressed like this, he's still a sick man and he's already had a full day.'

'If everything goes according to plan, he won't even know you're gone.'

'He's bound to,' she cried frantically. 'They'll be cutting the cake soon. He'll expect me to be there.'

'Kathleen will reassure him.'

'I don't see how she can.'

'I had a word with her and it's all arranged,' Keir said calmly.

'You mean she knows about this—this…'

'Abduction?' Keir suggested. 'Yes, she knows, though I'm happy to say she doesn't regard it in quite that light.'

'How does she regard it?'

'More as a rescue mission.'

'I don't need rescuing.'

'That's a matter of opinion.'

Remembering it was revenge he was after—on her for leaving him, on Martin for taking her—she said, 'But you don't think of it as rescuing me?'

'No, I think of it as reclaiming my own.'

Feeling like a bone being fought over by two snarling dogs, Sera shivered.

Making an effort to get back to the main point, she asked caustically, 'So how is Kathleen going to reassure Martin? Surely not by telling him I'm being *rescued*, and by you of all people.'

A little smile tugged at the corner of Keir's chiselled mouth. 'Hardly. What we arranged was this. When he realizes you're not there and gets restive, Kathleen will go to look for you. After a few minutes she'll come back and tell him that, because of the earlier upset, you've gone to bed early with a splitting headache. He'll surely remember you mentioning a headache? There are no elevators at Pine Cove, so he's unlikely to try and check for himself.'

Though relieved to some degree, Sera was overwhelmed by the hassle and futility of it all. Keir just didn't understand what he was up against.

Seeing the bleak look on her face, he said more gently, 'As well as his guests and a houseful of servants, Rothwell has Kathleen, don't forget. It isn't as though we're leaving him totally abandoned and helpless…'

That was true of course, but it wasn't the point. It was *her* Martin always wanted with him or, at the very least, close by.

If he ever found out that she had left the house in this underhand way, there would be hell to pay, and it would involve Kathleen too. So she must make sure he never did find out.

Hopefully, when Keir realized he was getting nowhere, he would take her back… Though it would have to be soon. There was a night security system that came into operation at sunset…

Staring down at the hands clasped in her lap, Sera was trying to work out how best to slip into the house and upstairs without being noticed, when he added, 'Believe me, he'll be fine. It'll probably be tomorrow lunch-time before he realizes you're not there.'

'Tomorrow lunch-time?' she echoed incredulously. 'You're not planning to keep me all night?'

'I'm planning to keep you for as long as it takes.'

Her eyes widened and struggling to swallow past the knot of fear that lay like a hard lump in her throat, she asked in a strangled voice, 'For as long as it takes to do *what*?'

'Oh, Sera, what big eyes you've got,' he mocked gently.

How could he tease her at a time like this? she wondered wildly.

But perhaps that was *all* he was doing? Maybe this had been planned as a small revenge against *her* for leaving him, rather than against Martin.

They were heading now towards the rural part of the island. Pines and beach roses lined the roadside, and the last oblique rays of the evening sun made the trees cast long dark shadows. In a short while the sun would be gone and it would start to get dusk.

Taking a deep breath, she asked carefully, 'You surely aren't intending to drive around all night?'

'No.'

'Then, what *are* you intending to do?'

Even as she spoke, she got a disturbing picture of Keir pulling the car into some quiet lane, taking her in his arms, making love to her...

He'd said he wanted her; he'd said it had been a long time...

A sidelong glance at her face had him shaking his head. 'No, that isn't what I had in mind,' he told her with a touch of derision. 'I'm no longer an impetuous youth, and not athletic enough to enjoy making love in a car. These days I like to take it slow and easy, to give and receive the greatest amount of pleasure. As far as I'm concerned that means the comfort of a bed and the maximum degree of privacy.'

Her cheeks burning, she bit her lip. After a moment she pointed out as evenly as possible, 'You still haven't answered my question.'

His voice full of irony, he said, 'I intend to take you somewhere out of the way and romantic. Somewhere we can have a bit of supper, enjoy a heart-to-heart talk and do anything else that we feel like doing...'

Trying to ignore the latter half of the sentence, she said coldly, 'You mean a motel of some kind.'

'Not on your life. For one thing, motel walls are usually paper-thin...'

His words caused little frissons of alarm to run up and down her spine.

'And I'd prefer us to be some place where we're quite alone and can't be overheard.'

'Such as?'

'Such as an old farmhouse in the middle of nowhere.'

His voice dropping to a husky purr, he went on, 'I want you as you were before, warm and soft and receptive, a passionate woman who found pleasure in what we were sharing, who shuddered with delight when I nuzzled my face against her breasts and—'

'Stop it!' she cried raggedly.

'Am I disturbing you?' he enquired innocently.

Struggling to get her agitation under control, she made one last desperate attempt to make him change his mind. 'Please, Keir, you must see that things aren't the same. You're wasting your time...'

'I hardly think so.'

'I'm engaged to Martin now.'

'You were engaged to Martin when I kissed you the other day, but your response was all I could have hoped for.'

'I—I had no intention of responding. You took me by surprise... I'll never be willing to make love with you.'

'We'll see, shall we?'

Shivering, she bit her lip and lapsed into silence.

Keeping to the country lanes, they went through a couple of small villages, past an old water-mill, and suddenly there was nothing around them but potato fields.

A pale moon was just rising and, in the eerie half-light Scots called the gloaming, the potato rows fanned out in serried ranks of lush green.

In the distance was a farmhouse, looking like a doll's house, its windows beaming with yellow light.

'Muntys' Farm. Our nearest neighbour,' Keir remarked casually, turning down a bumpy dirt road, little more than a track.

A moment or two later an old farmhouse, partially hidden by a semi-circular stand of tall trees, came into view. With its rust-brown shingled roof, what looked like arching eyebrows over the dormer windows, and a wooden veranda, it could have come straight from a fairy story.

The overgrown garden was full of colour—pink and purple azaleas, a riot of yellow roses, masses of deep red rhododendrons, sprawling bushes full of blue flowers Sera couldn't put a name to. Only the lawn had been trimmed and kept under some kind of control.

Leaving the car on the gravel drive, Keir got out and came round to open her door. It opened easily from the outside, she noted with irritation.

When he'd politely offered his hand to help her out, and had it ignored, he reached into the back and produced a sailcloth tote bag.

Sera looked sharply at it realizing that, if he really did intend to keep her here, she had nothing but what she stood up in.

No nightie, no toothbrush, no clean undies, nothing to wear in the morning. Though that faded into insignificance compared to her other problems.

She wondered briefly what any neighbours would have thought, to see two people in evening dress in this very rural setting.

Reading her mind, Keir said, 'Civilization is only a mile or so away. If the circumstances had been different we could have popped over to Joey's for a meal. As it is, we'll have to eat out of the icebox.

'After you.'

A hand at her waist, he urged her over a gravelled area and across the slatted wooden porch. From his pocket he produced a keyring with a couple of keys on it and, opening the door, flicked on the light.

Sera found herself in a spacious living-room with stairs

running up to the second floor. The rough plaster walls were white, and it was sparsely furnished with a black leather suite and a few pieces of country pine. There were brightly coloured rugs on the floorboards and thick woven curtains at the windows.

'As you can see, I haven't yet got round to doing anything with the place.'

'So you own it?'

'Yes, it's mine.'

Dropping the tote bag, he took off his evening jacket and tossed it over a chair, before removing his black bow-tie with great deliberation and putting it on the top of a nearby bookcase.

Suddenly apprehensive, Sera watched, dry-mouthed, while he began to undo his shirt buttons.

The top three undone, he paused and remarked mockingly, 'There's no need to look quite so scared, I'm not planning to leap on you before we're hardly through the door. As I said, I prefer the slow, leisurely approach and the comfort of a bed.'

As the colour rose in her cheeks, he suggested, 'Now, if you'd like to freshen up before supper?' Picking up the tote bag, he turned and led the way upstairs.

After a moment, her soft mouth compressed, Sera followed him, the wooden treads creaking at every step.

Opening a door on the right of the landing, he showed her into a white-walled room with a few brightly patterned rugs scattered on the black floorboards.

There was a big brass bedstead covered by a beautiful old patchwork quilt, its colours faded with time and laundering, a huge, old-fashioned wardrobe, and a massive, bow-fronted chest of drawers.

An old iron fireplace with a black grate dominated the

far wall, and the combined smells of soot and lavender hung on the still air.

'Not terribly luxurious, I'm afraid,' Keir remarked casually. 'But it's the only bedroom that's furnished. The house belonged to an elderly couple who had inherited it, and they only used it for the occasional weekend.'

All Sera had heard was 'it's the only bedroom that's furnished', and her heart began to throw itself against her ribs.

If he really did mean to try and seduce her, to claim back what he regarded as *his*, how ever would she find the strength to hold out against him?

CHAPTER SEVEN

'EARLIER tonight you mentioned a headache...' His voice broke into her agitated thoughts. 'Is it any better?'

'No.'

He opened a door to the left, showing a flash of pale pink tiles, and returned after a moment with a glass of water and two white tablets which he dropped into her palm. 'Take these, that should do the trick.'

She put them in her mouth, took a sip of water, and swallowed. They refused to go down and she shuddered as they dissolved bitterly on her tongue.

'All right?' he asked.

'Yes, thank you,' she managed.

'Then, I'll leave you to it. Ten minutes, shall we say?'

Sera recognized that despite the polite phrasing it was an instruction not to take any longer.

'Oh, by the way, if you want to take off the party gear, there's a change of clothing in the tote.'

It would look too much like *accepting* the situation, and she was about to refuse when, his eyes on the low-cut bodice of her dress, he added, 'Though I must say I much prefer what you have on at the moment.'

A second later the latch clicked behind him.

There was neither lock nor bolt on the door, so she couldn't simply lock herself in. Nor could she move the heavy furniture to form a barricade.

Hurrying over to the window she opened it and peered out. There was an easy drop to the sloping roof of the veranda but, judging by the condition of the wood, it wouldn't even bear her slight weight. If she fell through and hurt herself, she would be in an even worse mess.

There had to be a better way to escape...

But first she would have to change into something more suitable than an ankle-length evening dress. Though she would have changed anyway, after Keir's provocative remark...

Perhaps that was why he'd made it?

Opening the bag, she discovered several changes of dainty undies, a pair of well-cut white jeans, a button-through skirt, two silky shirts, a lightweight cashmere sweater, and a pair of flat-heeled sandals. There was also a nightdress, a dressing gown and a toilet bag stocked with everything she might conceivably need.

Keir had been very thorough.

The mere fact that he'd gone to so much trouble only served to re-emphasise that this abduction had been carefully planned.

Shivering, she took off her dress and undies and, deciding that it was too much of a risk to keep wearing it, removed the silver chain from around her neck.

Wrapping it in one of the shirts, she hid it carefully in the bottom of the bag before going to take a quick shower.

Some ten minutes later, dressed in jeans, the remaining shirt and the flat-heeled sandals, she made her way down the creaking stairs.

There was no sign of Keir and the front door beckoned.

Her hand was on the latch when common sense told her it would be useless to try and make a run for it. Once clear of the garden, with flat potato fields stretching as far as the eye could see, even in the half light she would be easy to spot.

With the car at his disposal, Keir would easily overtake her before she'd gone half a mile.

Unless *she* could take the car.

At this hour the roads would be fairly clear. If she could find her way back to Pine Cove before Martin missed her. she could pretend this whole thing had never happened.

Thinking back, she recalled that Keir had dropped the car keys into his jacket pocket and his jacket was where he'd left it, tossed casually over a chair.

Her heart in her mouth, she took out the keys and had turned to the door once more when she stopped dead. She had left the silver chain in the tote bag.

It would be a big risk to creep up and get it, but she couldn't bear to go without it... And if Keir found it, it would tell him too much. Possibly enough to make him renew his efforts to take her away from Martin.

The keys in her hand, she was heading back to the stairs, when her captor's voice asked suddenly, 'Changed your mind?'

She jumped violently and spun to face him.

Keir was lounging in the doorway of what was obviously the kitchen. He had changed into casual trousers, an open-necked shirt, and trainers.

'I'll take care of those.' He held out his hand and, reluctantly, she surrendered the keys, which he slipped into the pocket of his trousers.

There must be another bathroom, she realized, because his hair was still damp from the shower, and he was freshly shaven.

Despite herself, her eyes lingered on that beautifully chiselled mouth, and the beguiling cleft in the strong chin.

As though in response to that look, he ran lean fingers over his smooth jaw and remarked with soft intent, 'Stubble can wreak havoc on a flawless skin like yours.'

He watched with satisfaction while her eyes dropped in

confusion, before standing aside and ushering her through to the kitchen.

At first glance it appeared to be a typical farmhouse kitchen, with a stone floor, a huge black range and a scrubbed wooden table. But she was slightly surprised to see that, though the character of the place had been kept, it seemed to have most mod cons.

Opening the freezer cabinet, he took out a large, brightly coloured box. 'How about a pizza? That shouldn't take too long.'

'I'm not hungry,' she informed him flatly.

'Have you had anything to eat since lunch-time?'

'No,' she admitted. She hadn't had a great deal then. Ever since the accident, her appetite had been poor.

'Well, as it's never been part of my plan to starve you into submission, I'd like you to have something.'

When she half shook her head, he said, 'Of course if you *really* don't want to eat, we could always go straight to bed.'

She swallowed hard, while the apprehension his words provoked made a shiver run through her.

He raised a dark brow. 'So which is it to be?'

'I'd prefer the pizza.'

'Hardly flattering, but eminently sensible. You've lost more weight than I thought. The clothes I bought for you are the size you used to wear, but I see they're on the big side.'

Recalling his fury when Martin had bought clothes for her, she only just managed to suppress a barbed comment.

But mentally in tune, as usual, Keir remarked grimly, 'In this case it was justified.'

'On what grounds?'

'On the grounds that an evening dress is hardly the ideal item of clothing to be abducted in.'

When, biting her lip, she relapsed into silence, he shrugged and got on with the preparations for the simple meal.

As soon as a green salad had been tossed and the pizza placed in the oven, he suggested, 'We've time for a drink while it's cooking. What would you like?'

She would have liked to refuse but, facing the fact that it was foolish to remain thirsty, she said, 'Fruit juice, please.'

He poured two tall glasses chinking with ice and, having handed her one, opened the back door and led the way outside.

'I thought we'd eat on the porch so we can enjoy the moonlight.'

The rails of the old wooden veranda were twined around with gnarled and twisted grapevines and rambling roses. It had a lantern each side of the door and was furnished with a table and chairs as well as a swing-seat.

Sera was making for one of the upright chairs when, a hand beneath her elbow, Keir steered her to the swing-seat and sat down beside her. 'We might as well be comfortable.'

He had left the lanterns unlit and, out of range of the kitchen window, the porch was washed with silver moonlight.

It was warm and still, the balmy air full of night sounds and the night fragrances that are so much more poignant than those of the day.

They sat for a while sipping their drinks, neither saying a word. Then Keir turned to her and asked, 'How's the headache?'

'Much better, thank you,' she answered with studied civility.

When she said nothing further, as though set on making

polite conversation, he queried lightly, 'So what do you think of my new house? Do you like it?'

Normally she would have loved it, but in these circumstances it was just another prison.

She considered not replying. Then, unable to see the sense in making a bad situation worse, said evenly, 'It seems a strange choice.'

'I wanted a house on Long Island, within easy reach of the sea, but I didn't fancy a sumptuous place in the Hamptons surrounded by neighbours, well-kept lawns, and swimming pools. This kind of farmhouse, with real character, has become some of the most sought-after real estate on the island. More valued than contemporary property and, in my opinion, a great deal nicer. So when it came on to the market a short time ago I thought I'd take a look at it. I liked it on sight and decided to keep it.'

'For romantic weekends?' The words were out before she could prevent them. Hastily, she added, 'If I remember rightly, you used the word *romantic*...'

Hearing the hint of derision, he raised a dark brow. 'And you don't think it is? When you're sitting surrounded by moonlight and roses on the back porch of a place steeped in history...'

He uncoiled his considerable length with a sigh. 'We might as well eat. The pizza should be done by now.'

When he returned with a laden tray, she had moved to sit in one of the upright chairs by the table.

Keir nodded his approval. 'Having scared you into it, I'm glad to see you haven't changed your mind about eating.'

Lifting her chin, she lied, 'You didn't scare me into it...'

Seeing by his amused smile that he didn't believe a word, she added firmly, 'I found I was hungry after all.'

'Good.'

He helped her to half the pizza and a generous amount of salad, before pouring a glass of red wine for them both.

In resentful silence she picked up her knife and fork but, after her first mouthful, she realized her words had been truer than she'd thought.

After they'd done justice to the meal, he raised his glass in a toast. 'Here's to Kathleen, who made this possible.'

When, tight-lipped, Sera refused to drink, he said quietly, 'Don't hold it against her. Kathleen did what she did very largely for your sake. She thought it was for the best.'

'She was wrong! She should have considered Martin.'

'I think you'll find she *was* considering him. If you have a beloved, headstrong child, would you want that child to keep something you knew was going to hurt it?'

'The only way I'll hurt Martin is by going off with another man, by not being there when he wants me.'

'I guess she was thinking in broader terms. He's already got one failed marriage behind him. What about the future, when he's married to a woman he doesn't really love, and who doesn't love him?'

'But he *does* love me.'

'He's infatuated, obsessed, call it anything you like.... except love. If it was love, affection, even liking, something good would survive, something strong enough to glue the marriage together. But, sooner or later, both infatuation and obsession die, then what's left? Nothing but emptiness...'

He spoke with passion and conviction and she was forced to agree with him.

But it still didn't alter anything. Until Martin's feelings for her, whatever they were, died, she couldn't walk away from him. While he still wanted her, she owed it to him to stay.

There was a long pause, while Sera sat like a marble statue.

His long, heavy-lidded eyes on her face, Keir commented quietly, 'I could almost swear that you agree with what I've just said.'

'I do.'

With an odd note in his voice, he asked, 'But it doesn't make any difference?'

'No.'

As though too restless to sit still, he got to his feet and began to pace backwards and forwards.

'There's still time to take me back,' she suggested quietly.

She saw his teeth gleam as he smiled like a tiger. 'I don't give up that easily... Now, if you've had enough to eat, I'll make some coffee.'

He loaded the tray and carried it back into the house, while she sat staring blindly over the garden.

The moonlight had bleached the colour from the shrubs and flowers, leaving everything silvered and ethereal, while across the blue sky little puffs of grey cloud drifted like smoke signals...

Returning with the coffee, Keir asked, 'Would you like to move back to the swing-seat? It's a great deal more comfortable.'

She would rather have stayed where she was, but guessing that though the question had been politely phrased, it was more in the nature of a command, she obeyed.

His grin confirming that she'd been right, he remarked sardonically, 'My word, you *have* learnt to toe the line.'

In no way a violent person, Sera was seized by a sudden urge to take the smile off that handsome face with a good hard smack. But, recalling how he'd once said, 'Don't ever do that again', she somehow quelled the impulse.

Putting the tray on the table, he filled two cups from the steaming coffee pot and handed her one.

They remained silent until their cups were empty and he'd replaced them on the tray. Then, coming to sit beside her, Keir said on a note of quiet purpose, 'Now, I think it's time for that talk.'

'I've already told you there's nothing to say.'

'And I've made it plain that I don't agree. There are things I need to know. Questions I want answers to.'

She stood her ground. 'What if I don't choose to answer your questions?'

He shrugged. 'I've got plenty of time. I don't mind if it takes a week to get some answers.'

Knowing there was no way she could win against such a set purpose, she gave in. 'What do you want to know?'

'I want to know about your relationship with Rothwell. Why you stay with a man you don't love, a man who can be so cruel?'

'Martin isn't cruel...not really.'

Picking up her hand, Keir pointedly studied the marks on her slender wrist. 'Then, how would you describe deliberately bruising someone?'

'But he wouldn't have done it if you hadn't made him furious.'

'He shouldn't have done it then. Why take his anger out on you?'

'Martin wasn't always like this.' She made an effort to defend him. 'The accident changed him... He's been in a great deal of pain, and suffered a lot of anxiety and frustration—'

'I understand all that. I'm not some kind of callous monster. But you were injured as well. Why make you his whipping boy?'

'He doesn't,' she protested.

'Don't lie to me,' Keir said shortly. 'I'm well aware how he treats you. Before she realized I knew you, Kathleen told me quite a lot.'

'I suppose you got to know her deliberately?'

'Yes.' He made no bones about it. 'I'd been aware for a little while that something odd was going on at Anglo American. Rothwell was getting a reputation for being a recluse, and that isn't like him at all. Then I heard that he'd been involved in an accident of some kind, which gave me food for thought...

'I had the Warburton Building watched so that, by the time I moved in, I knew pretty well what the situation was. But I needed a fly on the wall view, so to speak.

'His nurse was the obvious choice, therefore I made it my business to get to know her. I discovered that, because her previous patient had lived in Washington, she had no friends in New York, so I took her for coffee and doughnuts whenever she had an odd hour off.

'It was no hardship. Kathleen's as pretty as she's practical. A thoroughly nice person... And devoted to Rothwell,' he added.

'We had some interesting talks. I don't mean she was indiscreet in any way, but the right kind of casual questions dropped in from time to time produced some very revealing answers.

'Reading between the lines, and taking into consideration what she *didn't* say, I got a pretty good picture of what's been going on. What I don't know, is why you put up with it.'

'If things were as bad as you're making out, I could have just walked away.'

'Why didn't you?'

Carefully, she said, 'Because they're *not* that bad.

Martin can be unkind at times, and demanding, but he isn't *cruel*.'

'That's a matter of opinion. I gather he allows you very little freedom.'

'He doesn't exactly keep me in chains.'

'But to escape for a little while you've been forced to sneak out of the apartment without his knowledge.'

She ran her tongue over dry lips. 'Because he's been so ill, he wants me to be there.'

'To take care of him?'

'Not exactly... Kathleen does that. He just doesn't like me out of his sight.'

'In case you leave him for good? He can't be very sure of you.'

When she said nothing, Keir changed tack. 'You told me you've been working from home as his PA?'

'Yes.'

'But he doesn't give you any wages?''

'No,' she admitted, her colour rising as she recalled the time she'd been forced to borrow a few dollars from Kathleen to buy some small personal item.

'But he provides me with my food and a roof over my head, a luxurious one at that, and he's urged me to buy anything I want and charge it to him.'

'And do you?'

After a moment, she shook her head.

'Why not?'

She spoke the exact truth. 'It doesn't seem fair when I'm giving him virtually nothing in return.'

'So, because you don't sleep with him, you're reluctant to spend his money... But I presume you'd spend it if you were married to him?'

'A wife is somewhat different from a fiancée... Though I'd be happy to keep on working if he wanted me to.'

'You mean be independent? I doubt if he'd want you to do that. His whole strategy is geared to keeping you dependent on him...'

Recognizing that as the truth, she made no attempt to argue.

'And, at a guess, I'd say you don't like it?'

'No, I don't,' she admitted shortly.

'So presumably that's why you were wearing the same dress you wore at the Anglo American party?'

'You saw so little of me that night, I'm surprised you remember.' Then quickly she added, 'I'm sorry, I didn't mean that like it sounds. I know now you couldn't help it.'

'I wish to God I had,' he burst out suddenly. 'If I'd stayed with you then, things might have worked out differently. You might have had my ring on your finger rather than his.'

'Then, you do believe it wasn't his money that influenced me?'

'I'm starting to.'

There was a long, thoughtful silence.

Attracted by the lighted window, a huge furry moth began to dash itself against the glass.

Sera winced at the soft thuds its body was making.

Without a word Keir got up and, opening the door a crack, switched off the light, leaving only the pale moon to illuminate the scene.

Released from that fatal attraction, the moth fluttered away.

'Thank you,' Sera murmured. 'That was kind of you.'

Taking his seat again, he said evenly, 'I hate to see any living thing set on a course of self-destruction. Life is much too precious to waste.'

He was right, of course. And *she* would be wasting her

life married to a man she didn't love, a man who didn't want children.

But what choice had she got…?

'Did you sleep with him before the accident?' Keir's question came out of the blue.

'What?' she asked, startled.

'I asked if you slept with Rothwell before the accident?'

'No. I've never slept with him.'

She heard Keir's faint but unmistakable sigh of relief. Then he asked sharply, 'Why not? You slept with me.'

'Perhaps I didn't want to seem promiscuous,' she retorted with a flash of spirit. 'Or maybe Martin has old-fashioned values…'

Keir put his own interpretation on that. 'Which means that finding you were…shall we say…not over eager, Rothwell didn't push too hard. He must have been afraid of scaring you off before you were married. Then the accident happened, and he's been waiting ever since. I could almost feel sorry for the poor devil…'

Pursing his lips, Keir added ruefully, 'In a sense, we're both in the same boat.'

Unsure what to make of that cryptic remark, Sera said, 'I don't know what you mean.'

'I mean that we're both frustrated, that for different reasons we've each been waiting the best part of a year for a woman we're both obsessed with…'

Two men, she thought bleakly, each of them wanting her, but neither of them loving her. It was terrifying to be the victim of *one* man's obsession let alone *two*…

Keir had loved her once, or so he'd said… But he'd allowed bitterness, and what he described as disillusionment, to warp his feelings.

Now, combined with a desire for her, was an even greater desire for revenge.

She shuddered and shuddered again.

Watching her, he returned to the attack. 'You still haven't answered my question. Why do you stay with him, Sera?'

'You must *know* why,' she said desperately.

Keir's black brows drew together in a frown. 'Tell me something,' he pursued after a moment, 'if it hadn't been for the accident would you have gone ahead and married him?'

Sensing a loaded question, she answered with what firmness she could muster, 'Of course I would.'

'You hadn't been having second thoughts?'

Without looking at him, she queried, 'What makes you ask that?'

'Something that Cheryl let slip. When I tried to pin her down she looked uncomfortable and said it was nothing really, she'd just had the feeling that you wanted out. Though her brother was mad about you, she wasn't convinced that you loved him. She'd thought at first it was *me* you loved. When you gave me the brush-off and began to go out with him, she decided it was the Rothwell millions that had attracted you, and said as much...'

Sera had never really understood why Keir had been so certain it was Martin's money she was after; now it seemed that Cheryl might have put the idea into his head.

'But Rothwell had set his heart on marrying you, and she thought that for the sake of having a rich husband you'd go through with it. Then, apparently, she began to change her mind... So what I'm asking is, had *you* changed *your* mind? Had you, Sera?' His dark eyes, silvered by the moonlight, pinned her. 'I want the truth.'

Worn down by his questions, his sheer persistence, and the knowledge that he wouldn't give up until he had got at the truth, she admitted heavily, 'Yes, I had changed my mind. I should never have agreed to marry him in the first place… But he was very likeable, and good company when I was lonely. He gave me his time, treated me as though I mattered more than his business, and I was grateful. I seemed to have lost—' About to say *you* she broke off abruptly and bit her lip.

His eyes on her face, Keir prompted, 'You seemed to have lost…?'

Swallowing, she went on doggedly, 'I seemed to have lost my desire for a career, and I suppose I persuaded myself that if I married Martin the gratitude and affection I felt for him would grow into love. We hadn't been engaged very long when I realized I'd made a bad mistake. I tried to tell him how I felt, but he refused to believe I was serious. He said it was just pre-wedding nerves.'

'So you let things drift?'

She sighed. 'For a while. Then I knew I just *had* to make a stand. I was planning to give him back his ring the weekend we were due to go to Pine Cove, the weekend of the accident, but nothing went right…'

Keir sat like stone, neither moving nor speaking, only his eyes alive in the mask of his face.

With a kind of dull hopelessness, she went on, 'If I'd broken the engagement *before* the accident happened, it would have been different. But I didn't, and afterwards it was too late. I couldn't just walk away from him when he was so badly injured.'

'So you're determined to marry a man you don't love?'

'There's nothing else I can do.'

Taking her hand, Keir said urgently, 'Don't be a fool, Sera. You can't sacrifice yourself like this.'

'Leave me alone,' she begged, jerking her hand free. 'I can't stand any more!'

'Just answer me one more question with absolute truth.

Did you agree to marry Rothwell because you thought I no longer cared about you?'

Barely above a whisper, she answered, 'Because I thought you never had.'

She saw the flare of triumph in his eyes before he asked sharply, 'How did you feel about me? Had you stopped loving me?'

'You said one more question, and I've answered it. Oh, please, Keir, take me back home. It's not too late.'

Reading his refusal in his face, she cried, 'Can't you see it's useless? I'll never leave Martin while he still wants me. Keeping me here is just a waste of time. Talking won't alter anything.'

'*Talking* might not.'

It was true, and she knew it.

If he once touched her intimately, kissed her, she would be lost. What she felt for Keir was stronger than guilt, more powerful than conscience...

But aware that she must keep fighting, she said raggedly, 'I'll never willingly sleep with you.'

He sighed. 'Then, I may have to try a little friendly persuasion. But I don't think it will be too difficult to get you to respond.'

'Even if, on a purely physical level, you can make me respond, it won't alter anything. You can't keep me here forever and as soon as you let me go I'll run back to him.'

'And what will you tell him?'

'The truth, if necessary.'

'He won't like the idea that you've slept with me—to put it mildly.'

'Oh, yes, I know he'll be furious, but I'll crawl on my knees if I have to...'

Her words had all the effect she could have hoped for.

She felt Keir stiffen and, without looking at him, knew he was shaken to the core.

But still it failed to deflect him from his purpose.

'And have him bruise you again?' he demanded harshly. 'Oh, no! If anyone is going to make bruises on you, it'll be me... But they'll be marks of passion rather than anger, and I'll enjoy kissing them better.'

His words provoked a turbulent sense of anticipation, causing her skin to grow heated and her heart to grow chilled.

Sweeping her up in his arms, he carried her into the house, shouldering the door shut behind them.

CHAPTER EIGHT

EVEN inside, the moonlight was so bright that he needed no other light while he made his way through to the living-room and climbed the creaking stairs.

Only too aware that it would be hopeless, Sera made no attempt to struggle. He was so much stronger than she was that words were her only defence and, so far, words had proved useless against his determination.

In the bedroom he put her down on the bed and slipped off her sandals. Then, in spite of her clutched hands and bitter objections, he unzipped her jeans, easing them over her hips and buttocks, and freeing her slender legs.

Sitting down beside her, he brushed a strand of fine black hair away from her cheek, before bending his dark head to drop a kiss on her forehead, the tip of her nose, then a series of soft, baby kisses on her lips.

Her eyes closed, she lay quite still, striving to marshal her defences, to disassociate herself from what was happening to her.

Deprived of sight, her other senses seemed heightened. She could hear his light, even breathing and the strong beat of his heart.

She found herself achingly aware of a sharp, clean scent that was purely male, the freshness of his breath, and the tang of his aftershave cologne.

Softly, tenderly, he kissed her face, her eyelids, her throat and then again her parted lips. His kisses were sweeter, more seductive, than anything she could have imagined.

Sera had braced herself for some kind of onslaught and his unexpected tenderness disarmed her completely. She made a small sound, halfway between a sigh and a sob.

'It's all right.' His voice was gentle, soothing. 'I won't hurt you.'

He might not hurt her physically, but if he made love to her against her will he'd break her heart. She wanted to tell him that, but no words would come.

As though he could read her mind, he said quietly. 'This is the one course left open to me. I can't seem to get through to you in any other way and, if only for the sake of what we once had, I've got to make you change your mind.'

But he couldn't make her change her mind. It wasn't that simple.

Watching her face, seeing her silent rejection of his words, he said slowly. 'A year ago I thought that you loved me. Did you, Sera? I need to know.'

She opened heavy eyes and looked up at him in the moonlight that made the room nearly as light as day.

Almost as if the words were dragged out of her, she whispered, 'Yes, I did love you.'

'And do you still?'

If she admitted that she did, all hope of winning the fight would be lost. And somehow she just *had* to win. Summoning every last ounce of will-power, she said, 'No.'

His head jerked a little, as though she'd struck him. Then he said quietly, 'Well, even if it makes you hate me, I refuse to stand by and watch you ruin your life.'

Lifting her left hand, he began to slide the half hoop of diamonds over her knuckle.

Like a poignant echo from the past, she recalled the time Martin had taken Keir's ring from her finger. Only this time it was like removing a shackle.

'Wh-why are you doing this?' The stammered words were a forlorn and belated protest.

Tossing it onto the bedside cabinet, he answered, 'I can't make love to you with another man's ring on your finger.'

'I don't *want* you to make love to me,' she cried, desperate to prevent him.

Softly and with complete certainty, he told her, 'You will in a little while.'

He resumed the seige, teasing and coaxing when she struggled to keep her mouth closed against him. His tongue tip followed the line of her lips, finding the soft, sensitive inner skin, encouraging them to part and, when they did, deepening the kiss until her head reeled.

While he kissed her, he undid the buttons of her shirt and the front fastening of her bra then, lifting her a little, deftly disposed of both garments, before lowering her back onto the pillows.

Her breasts were small and firm and beautifully shaped. He weighed and fondled them, caressing the petal-soft skin, before enclosing them in his hands, leaving only the nipples exposed to the warm and erotic ministrations of his tongue.

As he drew first one and then the other into his mouth, it brought such exquisite delight that she was unable to stifle the little whimpers and murmurs that rose in her throat.

When the sensations he was arousing got too much to bear, she ran her fingers into his thick, springy hair and tried to lift his head.

His response was to smooth a hand down her flat stomach to the scrap of ivory satin that was her only protection and, with the lightest of touches, draw all sensation down.

Feeling the jump and flutter of her tightly strung nerves

and muscles, he raised his head to kiss first her throat and then her lips.

Brushing his open mouth back and forth across hers, he slid his free hand under her hair to cradle her head and lift it into his kiss.

She made a small sound, almost like a moan, as his tongue explored and revelled in the moist sweetness of her mouth.

While he kissed her, his moving hand becoming dissatisfied, needing to replace the smooth satin of her briefs with the warm silk of her skin, he disposed of the last dainty barrier.

Then his long, sensitive fingers brushed downy curls, stroked along the smooth skin of her inner thigh and began a gentle and rhythmic exploration.

Her breath started to come in quick, uneven gasps, her heart raced, her whole body tensed and all coherent thought vanished.

Judged to perfection, his caress stopped just short, leaving her poised on the brink.

From a very long way away, she heard his voice ask, 'Well, Sera? Do you want me to make love to you?'

As though his determined mastery of her body had released her mind from its self-imposed restraints, she knew that the only thing that really mattered was this man: his voice, his touch, his taste, his scent in her nostrils...

Tonight she had run through the whole gamut of emotions: fear, anger, despair. Such deep feelings had stripped her bare, left her vulnerable and heightened her emotional capacity.

Through a tight throat, she said, 'Yes.' The single word sounded tortured.

'Are you quite sure about that?'

'Yes, I'm sure.'

This man was the man she loved and, after the last desolate year, it wasn't mere bodily satisfaction she craved, but warmth and comfort, at the very least a *semblance* of caring to fill her empty heart.

She wanted to feel his weight, hold him in her arms, cradle his dark head to her breast and, afterwards, go to sleep with her head pillowed on his shoulder.

Her slender body bathed in moonlight, she held out her arms to him.

Just for an instant he hesitated, touched by a fleeting sense of misgiving, a doubt that he was doing the right thing.

But she wanted him in a way she had never wanted Rothwell, he was certain of it…

And he needed to become a part of her, to make her part of himself, even if it meant he would never again be whole without her.

It took only a matter of seconds for him to strip off his own clothes and join her on the bed.

She gave a little sigh, and his, more than her own, welcomed him as she had done once before. He was the other half of herself, completing the whole, making sense of her being.

As though in perfect agreement with that unspoken thought, he said fiercely, 'You're mine, and you always will be.'

With his first strong thrust, the tightness in her abdomen eased and relaxed into incandescence and, when he began to move, a core of heat like a beating heart became a rhythm that caught her up and carried her along, as right and natural, as *necessary* as her own breathing.

Then the spiralling warmth and joy reached a climax and exploded inside her. Fierce, elemental torrents of feeling went surging through her to shoot triumphantly sky-high like molten lava.

The experience was shattering, mind-blowing, terrifying in its intensity.

She cried out his name and, as though he understood exactly what she was feeling, he answered thickly, 'Yes, I know, my love. I know.'

As their breathing and pulse-rate gradually returned to normal, he reached to pull the quilt over them. Within seconds, held securely in his arms, she was asleep.

Towards dawn, when she was warm and relaxed, her cheek resting just above his heart, he kissed her into wakefulness and made love to her again.

This time his lovemaking was slower and more contented, making a commitment rather than a statement.

What it lacked in fiery passion it made up for with a deep tenderness. He found ways then to tell her without words how beautiful she was, how rare and precious, how much pleasure she gave him.

When it was over and she was lying in his arms, his chin on her hair, one hand cupping her breast, his languorous thoughts drifting ahead, he asked, 'Where would you like to live?'

'Live?' she echoed as though emerging from a trance into the real world.

'I presume you won't want to stay in the Penthouse, so I thought I'd let Rothwell have it as a kind of consolation prize... That is, if he still wants it.'

He felt her whole body stiffen and, with a sudden sharpness, he asked, 'You can't still mean to go back to him?'

She pulled herself out of his arms and struggled to sit up. 'I have to.' Though her voice held anguish, it also held a determination that frightened him.

'After everything we've just shared?' he demanded harshly.

'I told you that I'll never leave Martin while he still wants me.'

Sitting beside her, he ran a hand through his tumbled black hair. No, he couldn't believe it. *Wouldn't* believe it.

Through his teeth, he said, 'I won't let you go.'

'You can't stop me, unless you intend to try and keep me a prisoner indefinitely. And you know as well as I do that isn't possible.'

He changed tack. 'Are you sure Rothwell will *want* you back after what's happened?'

Knowing how Martin had lied and cheated to get her, Sera had no doubt. 'Yes, I'm sure. As you said yourself he's obsessed with me.'

'No one can be responsible for someone else's obsession. Then roughly he said, 'Damn it, Sera, if you hold yourself responsible for *his* obsession, you'll have to hold yourself responsible for *mine*.'

She half shook her head. 'I don't hold myself responsible for any man's obsession. It's not that.'

'Then, what is it? Surely spending the night in my bed has altered things. When he knows—'

'For his sake, I hope he won't have to know anything,' she broke in a shade wildly. 'If you take me back before he misses me...'

'I'll never willingly take you back... And if you go back and *don't* tell him, I may have to.' Though it was mildly worded, it was undoubtedly a threat.

'But that will only mean hurting him for nothing... It won't make any *difference*.'

'I can't believe that spending the night in my bed won't have made *some* difference.'

'It's made everything a great deal more difficult, but it

hasn't *altered* anything. Martin's still in a wheelchair, and I'm certain he still wants me.'

'Just because he wants you it doesn't mean you have to go.'

Her despair evident, she cried. 'But how can I leave him when he's crippled? I'd never have another happy minute. It would be on my conscience until the day I died.'

'But he won't *be* crippled, you said so yourself.'

'His doctors *think* he'll be all right, but nothing's certain. They may be wrong. He may have more problems in store than they know.'

'The fact that he may have problems in store isn't a good enough reason to make you marry a man you don't love. You've given him all these months, stood by him through the worst. Now it's time you thought of yourself...'

Seeing by her set face that his words were having no effect, Keir seized her hands in a painful grip. 'Listen to me, Sera, it isn't as though the accident was your fault.'

He watched every trace of colour drain from her face leaving it like alabaster in the moonlight.

'But that's just it...' her words held a world of despair '...it *was* my fault. I'm the one responsible for putting him in that wheelchair, the one who's caused him all these months of pain and suffering... *Now* do you see why I can't leave him?'

Completely overwrought, she burst into tears.

Kier took her in his arms, cradling her head against his muscular chest. 'Don't cry, my love, don't cry.'

Rocking her, one hand moving soothingly up and down her spine, he murmured little disjointed words of comfort while he stared blindly over her head.

Of course. He should have seen it coming. The fact that she thought herself to blame made sense of her determination to stay with Rothwell, sense of her guilty need to sacrifice herself…

When the storm of emotion was over and she'd cried herself out, he reached for the box of tissues on the cabinet and mopped her up as though she was a child.

Then, settling her more comfortably across his lap, he kissed her blotched face and suggested quietly, 'Perhaps you'd better tell me all about it.'

She gave a little hiccuping sob. 'There's not a lot to tell.'

'Let me hear what there is.' When still she hesitated, he probed, 'What makes you think it was your fault?'

'Because I was driving.'

Jolted, he asked, 'Why were you driving?'

'Martin wanted me to. He told me he'd bought the car as a wedding present for me and he insisted that I should try it out… Knowing I was going to break the engagement, I felt terrible about it. But I couldn't say anything because Cheryl was there.'

'Did she go with you?'

'Yes.' Sera's voice was scarcely above a whisper.

Against his chest her body felt limp and boneless, a dead weight of despair. Keir's arms tightened round her. 'Go on, my love.'

'I didn't want to drive. I was on edge and nervous because I'd intended to give him back his ring and not go to Pine Cove, but everything had gone wrong and I hadn't had a chance to talk to Martin alone…'

'So what happened exactly?'

'We were almost there. We'd left the highway and were heading for the coast when I lost control on a sharp bend…'

She took a deep, shuddering breath. 'We veered off the

road and hit a tree. The car turned over and rolled down an embankment...'

'What happened to Cheryl?'

'She was sitting in the back and escaped with minor cuts and bruises, thank God... When I regained consciousness she came to see me in the hospital and told me about Martin.'

'How long were you unconscious?'

Sera put a hand to her head. 'Almost five weeks... And even when I did wake up my mind was confused.'

'In what way?'

'When I first came to, I felt convinced that I'd given Martin back his ring.'

Keir frowned. 'What makes you so sure you hadn't?'

'Because I was still wearing it. The hospital had taped over it.'

'Yet you seem to remember the accident clearly?'

'No. I don't remember it at all. Cheryl told me what had happened... The last thing I can recall is driving along the highway...'

Her voice was leaden with weariness and despair, her swollen eyelids almost closed.

He slid down the bed, taking her with him and, pillowing her head on his shoulder, cradled her while her breathing settled once more into the evenness of sleep...

Sera's brain stirred into life slowly, unwillingly. Lying with her eyes closed, she tried to sink back into blessed oblivion, but the waking process had begun and she couldn't stop it.

Though her thoughts were muddled and disjointed, one part of her mind was already aware that she didn't want to have to face whatever the coming day held...

But that kind of feeling was nothing new, it had been part of her life for a long time now.

As her brain cleared somewhat, she realized it must be quite early. Everything was quiet and still, both inside and out.

There was no movement, none of the usual sounds. No hum of air-conditioning, no faint rumble of traffic on Fifth Avenue, no noise of Manhattan stirring into life.

It took a few seconds more before she remembered that she wasn't in Manhattan; they had come down to Pine Cove for Martin's birthday. He was having a party...

Had *had* a party... And *Keir* had turned up...

He'd taken her to an old farmhouse, had carried her up the moonlit stairs and, in an austere, white-walled bedroom, had made love to her...

But surely it was just a dream? She'd dreamt of him making love to her so many times...

No, this was no dream. The memories were too vivid, too *real* to be only a dream...

And her own body confirmed that conclusion. Though tender in places, it was eminently content and satisfied. It was her mind that was in turmoil.

She sat up with a jerk in the big, double bed, making her head spin sickeningly. It was broad daylight and the space beside her was empty, though the pillow next to hers bore the imprint of Keir's head.

Her heart thumping wildly, she glanced towards the bathroom. The door was slightly ajar and there wasn't a sound.

Perhaps he was in the other bathroom, or downstairs making breakfast?

His clothes had vanished, she noticed, but hers were lying neatly over a chair. Her cheeks grew hot as she recalled with what ease he'd stripped them from her.

But gone was all the singing happiness and joy she'd felt then, the overwhelming delight of being in his arms once more.

All she could feel now was a fierce and futile resentment towards Keir for deliberately seducing her in spite of knowing how hard she was striving to be loyal to Martin.

But, after a moment or two, an ingrained honesty insisted that she couldn't lay all the blame at his door. He'd said he wouldn't use force and she'd believed him implicitly. If she'd said *no*, and *meant* it, it would never have happened.

He hadn't won the battle. It was her inability to hold out against him that had lost it.

She felt a burning shame, a fierce self-loathing, a swingeing contempt for her own weakness.

But it was too late for regrets.

What would Keir do now? Would he be willing to take her straight back to Pine Cove?

He'd remarked that she probably wouldn't be missed until lunch-time... So if he was still in the softer mood her tears had engendered the previous night, there might be a slim chance of getting back without Martin knowing, or ever having to know...

She glanced at her watch and was shocked to find it was almost eleven-thirty. No, surely it couldn't be that late?

But the curtains hadn't been drawn the previous night and, through the dormer window, she could see that the sun was already riding high in the cloudless blue sky.

As she pushed back the bedclothes, the sight of her bare hand reminded her that Keir had removed her ring. Weighed down by a leaden sense of inevitability, she reached for it and slid it on again.

Then, regaining her sense of urgency, she hurried into the bathroom and showered and cleaned her teeth as quickly as possible, before dragging a brush through her long hair.

Leaving the silky mass loose around her shoulders, she pulled on her clothes and, having retrieved the silver chain, put it on beneath her shirt and went swiftly down the stairs.

In the kitchen, a glass jug of coffee was keeping hot, but there was no sign of Keir, and the house had a deserted, empty feel to it.

A hasty tour of the place confirmed that it was indeed empty, but one of the bedrooms, furnished only with only a chest of drawers and a hanging rail, contained several changes of his clothes.

In the adjoining bathroom, damp towels, the lingering scent of shower gel and drops of water on the patterned glass of the shower cubicle showed that it had been in use not too long before.

It was a lovely day. Perhaps he was out on the veranda, or in the garden?

Running downstairs again, she pulled open the back door and looked out. There was no one on the porch apart from a sleek black cat with eyes like green glass, who was sitting on the sunny slats blinking drowsily.

Apparently quite at home, he rose to his feet and stretched, stiff-legged and straight-tailed, before coming to wind invitingly round her ankles.

'Well, hello.' Stooping briefly to rub behind his velvet ears, Sera asked, 'So who do you belong to? I'm sure you don't live here.'

As though in answer, he gave a miaow.

The pleasantries over, she left him there and began to walk quickly round the veranda. She'd only gone a few paces when, with a little run, he came pattering after her, purring like a rusty saw.

When she reached the front of the house there was still

no trace of Keir and, with a little shock of surprise, she saw his car was no longer standing where he'd left it.

She hadn't heard it drive away, but then, her bedroom was on the opposite side of the house.

With a queer, abandoned feeling, she wondered where he'd gone. What had been pressing enough to make him go off and leave her still sleeping?

Then, more urgently, she wondered, how long he was likely to be. If he didn't return soon she would lose any chance of getting back to Pine Cove before she was missed.

Just as the worrying thought crossed her mind, she heard the sound of an approaching car and, a few seconds later, the white Mercedes appeared from behind the screen of trees and pulled into the drive.

It was covered with dust, she noted abstractedly as the door swung open and Keir climbed out.

Dressed in smart but casual trousers and a blue shirt open at the neck, he looked fit and virile and heart-breakingly handsome.

Remembering everything that had taken place the previous night, Sera's cheeks grew hot and, despite all the questions buzzing around in her head, she found herself with nothing to say.

'Good morning.' Though he spoke pleasantly, he could have been greeting a total stranger, and his dark blue eyes held a look that she could only describe as impersonal.

She wasn't sure what she'd expected, but it hadn't been this cool detachment and, somehow, it threw her.

As the cat left her side to greet him, he added, 'I see you've made friends with Pyewacket.'

Pulling herself together with an effort, she asked, 'Then, he is yours?'

'No, he's just visiting. He lives at Munty's Farm.'

Reaching into the car, Keir produced a brown paper bag of provisions. 'Now, how about some lunch?'

Taking a deep breath, she said without preamble, 'I haven't time for lunch. I need to get back.'

With studied care, Keir removed the keys from the ignition and put them into the pocket of his trousers. 'All in good time. First I think we both need something to eat… And Pye will never forgive me if I don't produce his usual saucer of cream.'

The crackly bag under his arm, the cat at his heels, he turned to stroll in the direction of the kitchen.

It seemed that things weren't going to be as easy as she'd hoped. Hurrying after him, Sera pointed out anxiously, 'But if I don't go soon Martin is sure to realize I've gone missing, and that will cause endless trouble.'

'You've no need to worry,' Keir said evenly. 'Kathleen is very quick-witted. I'm sure she'll find some way to stall him.'

Putting the brown paper carrier on the kitchen table, he began to unpack it with unhurried precision… A newly baked loaf of bread, a carton of cream, a pack of eggs, some fresh oranges and grapefruit…

'But what if he discovers from the maid that my bed hasn't been slept in?' Sera burst out in mounting agitation. 'He knows I've no money and nowhere to go… Suppose he calls the police?'

'I told you, you've no need to worry.' Keir spoke with quiet authority. 'I'll deal with any problems that might arise.'

He pulled out one of the barrel-backed wooden chairs. 'Now, why don't you sit down and relax?'

The look on his face, even more than his words, made her realize that he had no intention of being rushed. If he did take her back it would be in his own good time, and on his terms.

Seeing nothing else for it, she reluctantly took a seat. As soon as she was settled, Pyewacket jumped into her lap and, paddling with his front paws, arched his back and pushed his furry head beneath her chin while he waited for his saucer of cream.

CHAPTER NINE

KEIR poured out a saucer of cream for the cat and said, 'Come on, Pye.'

The command was scarcely necessary. As soon as the saucer was placed on the floor, the cat jumped down and began to lap with delicate greed. When all the cream was gone, with regal dignity he retired to the porch to wash his whiskers and make his toilet.

Looking as though he had all the time in the world, Keir squeezed two glasses of fresh fruit juice and handed one to Sera.

Though he made no comment, she knew he had noticed that Martin's ring was back on her finger. Looking away from his level gaze, trying to appear composed, she said stiffly, 'Thank you.'

While she drank the juice, he put slices of ryebread in the toaster and whipped up a basin full of eggs.

Though the toast was crisp and the scrambled eggs deliciously light and fluffy, her stomach tied in a knot at the nerve-racking delay, Sera had to force down every mouthful.

They ate in silence and, when their plates were empty, Keir poured the coffee. While Sera fairly gulped hers, he drank his own at a leisurely pace that frayed her nerves even further.

Finally, unable to sit still a moment longer, she jumped up and offered, 'Shall I clear away?'

'There's no need. If I let Mrs Munty have the key she'll come over and do it. She changes the bed, stocks the fridge, and generally takes care of the place for me, as she did for the previous owners.'

With a glance at his watch, he rose to his feet, remarking, 'I'll just fetch the bag, then we can get going, if you're ready?'

Gritting her teeth, she answered as evenly as possible, 'Yes, I'm ready.'

After a moment or two he returned carrying the tote bag and said, 'We'll drop the key in on the way.'

It seemed he had no intention of coming back here.

Closing the kitchen door behind them, he addressed Pyewacket, who was just finishing grooming his tail. 'Fancy a ride home, Pye?'

The cat followed them round to the car and, as soon as the door was opened, jumped in and settled himself on the back seat.

'You'd think he understood every word,' Sera remarked, relief that they were finally getting under way loosening her tongue.

'I'm sure he does,' Keir responded. Then, as though following her lead and stirring himself to make polite conversation, he added, 'Apparently he comes from a long line of witches' cats.

'But, apart from that, he enjoys a ride. One time, when I hadn't realized he'd got into the car, I took him all the way back to New York with me...'

When they reached the neighbouring farm, via a bumpy track, Keir brought the car to a halt and climbed out.

Jumping into the front, Pye rubbed himself against Sera's legs then, tail erect, followed him, just as a fair-haired, sturdily built woman appeared from one of the barns.'

'I thought I heard a car,' she said cheerfully. 'Leaving for home already, Mr Sutherlands?'

'Yes.' Handing her the keys, he added, 'I don't expect to be back for a while, so if you could take care of things as usual?'

Her interest in his passenger barely concealed, she answered, 'Of course. Just let me know when you'll be wanting fresh supplies.'

'I'll do that. Many thanks.' With a little salute, Keir slid back behind the wheel and, a moment later, they were heading down the dusty track.

His long, well-shaped hands resting lightly on the wheel, a slight furrow between his black brows as though his thoughts were troubled, Keir headed for the coast in silence.

When they reached Pine Cove, would he just drop her off and go? Sera wondered. She wanted to ask him, to *beg* him to do just that. But afraid to broach the subject, she bit her lip and said nothing.

The day was hot and sunny and, preferring fresh air to air-conditioning, Keir was driving with the car windows down. The warm, sun-laden breeze ruffled his short black curls and blew Sera's long hair into a tangled mass of silk.

As they got nearer to the coast, it became built up and a great deal busier, and mingled with the scent of pine trees and roses was the salt tang of the sea.

Sera braced herself. They must be almost there now, but the road they were on was quite unfamiliar.

Feeling a sudden stab of apprehension, she asked, 'Are you sure this is the way to Pine Cove?'

'We're not going to Pine Cove,' Keir stated flatly.

She caught her breath and her heart started to race in alarm. 'But you...you *promised* to take me back.'

He lifted a black brow. 'I don't recall *promising* anything of the kind. If I remember rightly, what I said was,

''All in good time.'' The only promise I made was that I would deal with any problems that might arise.'

Urgently, she cried, 'But there might not *be* any problems if you'd only take me straight back and drop me in the lane.'

'Do you really imagine that, having abducted and seduced you, I'd just drop you off and walk away?'

'But you *must* see that it's for the best!'

'I can see that *you* think it would be, but I don't happen to agree.'

There was a silence while Sera struggled for self control. When she thought she could trust her voice, she asked jerkily, 'If we're not going to Pine Cove, where are we going?'

'Fiddler's Cottage.'

'Fiddler's Cottage? But surely that's where Cheryl and Roberto live... Why are we going there?'

'Because Cheryl asked me to take you.'

'I don't understand... Did she ask you last night at the party?'

'No, I called in to see her earlier this morning. She wanted me to bring you straight over then, but Roberto reminded her that they had been invited to a neighbour's house for lunch. However, they should be back home by now.'

Catching hold of the thing that seemed to matter most, Sera croaked, 'So she knows about...'

'About me abducting you? Yes, I told her.'

That wasn't precisely what she'd intended to ask. 'Does she know that...that...' Cheeks flaming, Sera stammered to a halt.

Slanting her a glance, Keir said wryly, 'I haven't told her we slept together, but I imagine she's drawn her own conclusions.'

Sera groaned. Now the fat was well and truly in the fire. Cheryl loved her brother and would hate to think he'd been treated so shabbily.

'Oh, why did you have to tell her anything? She'll never forgive me…'

'It might well be the other way around.'

Sera was just wondering what to make of that cryptic remark when they turned into the driveway of one of the rustic Cape Cod-style dwellings that were so sought after by wealthy New Yorkers.

A house plaque decorated with picture of one of the male fiddler crabs that roam the Hamptons' beaches, told her they had reached their destination.

The Mercedes had scarcely swung round on the apron before Cheryl left her seat on the veranda and came hurrying over.

Dressed in white slacks and a turquoise top, her red-gold hair gleaming in the sun, she made an attractive picture. But her face seemed strained, her sparkling happiness of the previous night, temporarily dimmed.

Her pale blue eyes anxious, she looked at Keir. 'Have you…?'

He shook his head. 'I thought it ought to come from you.'

Usually the two women exchanged hugs but, this time, there was a feeling of restraint, and neither made any move.

After a brief, but telling, hesitation, Cheryl asked, 'Would you prefer to sit inside or out?'

Gathering herself, Sera answered, 'Whichever you prefer.'

'Then, let's make it the porch.' Cheryl led the way across the veranda to a group of well-padded chairs each with its own adjustable parasol.

Keir waited politely until both the women were seated, then sat down next to Sera.

'I've left Roberto over at the Simpsons',' Cheryl said. 'The men were eating ice cream and discussing sport.' Awkwardly, she added, 'And, as he feels so very strongly about the whole thing, I thought it might be easier without him here.'

Sera felt sick inside. 'I'm sorry... I like Roberto, and I hate the idea of you both being so angry with me—'

'If you're talking about last night, you've nothing to be sorry for,' Cheryl broke in firmly. 'Keir has already explained that you had no choice in the matter... And it isn't *you* Roberto's angry with. It's *me*.'

As Sera gaped at her, she said, 'Look, it might be easier if I start right at the beginning.

'From the instant Martin first laid eyes on you he's been besotted. I've never known him to be so mad about any woman.

'The night of the Anglo American party, I could see the way he was fairly drooling over you. He gave me a look...' her mouth twisted wryly '...and, like any good sister, I took Keir away deliberately to give him a chance to be alone with you...

'Mind you, at that time, I had a personal interest in the outcome, but I soon discovered that as far as Keir was concerned, no other woman but you existed. Then, when Roberto persuaded me to stay that night... Well, we just hit it off... I don't need to tell you the rest...

'But to get back to the point... At first I thought you genuinely loved Keir and that Martin was wasting his time. Then you seemed to give Keir the brush-off, and I decided I could be wrong.

'Of course, Martin's a good-looking devil and, as far as most women are concerned, he's got what it takes. Yet I still wasn't convinced you were in love with him. The logical conclusion seemed to be that it was his money that attracted you.'

Seeing the look on Sera's face, she said quickly, 'I'm sorry, but I'm trying to be absolutely honest. Anyway, I made up my mind that, whichever it was, I'd keep out of it. Martin's no fool, and if he still wanted to marry you, well, it was up to him.

'As the wedding day got closer, I noticed that you were looking more and more unhappy. At that point I mentioned it to Martin. But he was so obsessed that all he could think about was getting a wedding ring on your finger before you changed your mind.

'"It'll be all right when we're married," he kept saying. "Sera isn't the kind of woman to go back on her word. As soon as she's my wife she'll settle down. I'll give her everything she's ever wanted."

'But I could see he was afraid. The only reason he bought that car was to try and keep your interest—'

'I don't know why you're telling me all this now,' Sera cut in desperately. 'It just isn't relevant any longer.'

'That part might not be, but the rest certainly is. I should have told you before. I've been feeling guilty for a long time now...'

'Guilty?' Sera exclaimed. 'Why on earth should *you* feel guilty?'

'Keep listening,' Cheryl said with a hint of dry humour, 'and you'll soon know.

'You remember the day of the accident, how Martin bullied you into driving?'

'He didn't exactly *bully* me,' Sera protested.

'OK, let's say he talked you into it. I could see you didn't want to. You looked tired and edgy.

'But it was a nice little car, the kind of thing most

women would have traded their eye-teeth for and, presuming you'd be delighted with a wedding gift like that, Martin had purposely given Carlson the weekend off.

'You'd once mentioned that though you'd never actually *owned* a car, you enjoyed driving, and I suppose he thought that if you got behind the wheel and had a taste of what he could offer you...' Letting the sentence tail off, Cheryl sighed.

Then, with a determined lift of the chin, she carried on, 'After the accident, when you asked me what had happened, the last thing you could remember was being on the highway. I take it you haven't remembered any more?'

'No.'

'Well, when I *told* you what had happened, for Martin's sake, I left quite a lot out.' She took a deep, almost shuddering breath.

Concerned, Sera said quickly, 'Are you sure you want to talk about it? This is no time to be getting yourself worked up.'

'I need to get it off my conscience,' Cheryl said decidedly. She patted her still flat stomach. 'Little Roberto will thrive all the better for it.'

'Well, if you're certain...?'

'Quite certain.' After a quick glance at Keir who, his dark face expressionless, had been sitting listening in silence, she went on, 'After we left the highway, Martin began talking about the honeymoon he'd planned. He suggested that you could extend it for a couple of weeks and take in Sydney after you'd left Hawaii.

'He'd got as far as, "We can spend longer in Australia if you want to. See the red heart..." when you burst out, "It's no good, Martin. I can't marry you. I'm sorry, but it's all been a dreadful mistake. I've tried more than once to tell you, but you kept saying it was just pre-wedding nerves, and it *isn't*..."'

Listening with almost feverish concentration, Sera's hands were clenched tightly together in her lap, the knuckles showing white.

'I think this time he knew you meant it, and he got terribly agitated. It was awkward for me. I'd rather not have been there.

'As though he suddenly remembered I was, he cried, "Stop the car. We can't talk like this."

'You drew off the road and stopped under some trees. Then the pair of you got out and he almost hustled you away.

'Though you were out of earshot, I could tell you were arguing. You seemed to be in tears and Martin looked almost frantic.

'I saw you take off your ring and try to hand it to him. He refused to take it and, in the end, you dropped it at his feet and walked away.

'His face livid, he picked it up and shoved it into the pocket of the linen jacket he was wearing...'

'So I *did* give him back the ring,' Sera whispered.

Without pausing to answer, Cheryl rushed on, 'You'd just reached the car when he came storming up. He pushed you out of the way and got behind the wheel himself...'

Sera's face was like chalk, her indrawn breath a sob.

'You'd barely had time to get in the passenger side and shut the door when he shot off.

'He wasn't in his right mind. He should never have been driving. Neither of you were wearing your seat belts.

'Before I had a chance to reason with him we got to the steep bend at Dunton Hollow. He was going far too fast and lost it. We hit a tree with terrific force, bounced off and went rolling down the embankment into a field.

'The car settled upside down. Its front was all crushed in and mangled; the back wasn't so bad. There was a surprising amount of noise: metal grating, glass crunching, steam hissing...

'I could smell petrol and I was terrified it was going to burst into flames. Even though I was groggy, I managed to unfasten my seat belt, but the doors were jammed and crumpled and I couldn't get out.

'After a few seconds of sheer panic, I got a hold of myself. My mobile was still working, thank God, and I phoned for the emergency services.

'Then I tried to see if I could do anything for you and Martin. You were lying all twisted up with blood on your face. I thought for a moment you were dead, but then I found a pulse and I could hear you breathing with difficulty.

'Martin was conscious, but he was trapped, unable to move. I asked him if there was anything I could do.

'He said hoarsely, "Feel in my pocket... The ring... Put it back on Sera's finger. She can't leave me. I won't let her."

'I wasn't sure whether he knew what he was saying, but when I didn't immediately do as he asked he started to cry and begged, "Oh, please, Sis, please... Do it for me."'

Cheryl stopped speaking abruptly, and her eyes filled with tears that threatened to overflow. 'He hadn't called me Sis for years.'

Her own eyes suspiciously bright, Sera reached impulsively for the other woman's hand and gave it a squeeze.

Dashing away the tears, Cheryl said, 'For heaven's sake don't be kind to me; I don't deserve it...'

Then, apparently determined to finish her story, she went on, 'I managed to find the ring and put it back on your finger. By that time the pain had hit Martin.

Perspiration was running down his face and he was groaning. I held his hand.

'Then he whispered, "There's something else; when the police get here, don't tell them I was driving."

'It was only six months since he'd barely escaped being convicted for dangerous driving. That's why he'd taken to going everywhere in the limousine instead of driving himself, which he'd always preferred.

'I said something like, "But they're sure to find out. When Sera comes to, she'll tell them."

'Martin insisted, "She won't if you ask her not to. Promise you'll ask her. The police won't push it. It isn't as if anyone else was involved."

'So I promised. In the event, I didn't need to ask you, because you wakened up convinced that you had been driving.

'I'm sorry. Sorry for everything. I should have told you the truth... But Martin clung to you so, and I hated the thought of letting him down.

'Though you looked far from happy, you seemed to be coping, and I told myself you were a grown woman, not a child, you didn't *have* to stay with him, if you didn't want to.

'I suppose in my heart of hearts I knew it was a feeling of guilt that kept you there. I'm sorry.' Again, her light blue eyes filled with water.

Sera, who had been sitting as motionless as a statue, watching the older woman's face, said quickly, 'Please, don't upset yourself...for the baby's sake, if nothing else.'

Cheryl made a valiant effort at composure. 'I just wish I'd told you sooner.'

'I don't understand why you've told me now,' Sera admitted.

'I've been wanting to for a while. I was so happy myself

I hated the thought of anyone else being unhappy, but it always came back to Martin and, each time, I chickened out.

'Then Keir came here this morning. He told me what action he'd taken and added that he had no intention of letting you go back to Martin until he knew "the cage door was open."

'He took me by surprise and my first instinct was to stonewall... But he soon made it clear that he already suspected something of what I've just told you and he insisted on knowing the whole truth.

'He looked so formidable I wouldn't have dared not tell him...' Biting her lip, she added, 'In my own way I'm a terrible coward. I dread the thought of Martin finding out that I've betrayed him...'

'As far as I'm concerned he won't know you've told me anything,' Sera promised.

'Thank you.' Once again emotion threatened to overwhelm the older woman.

There was a silence before she gathered herself enough to ask, 'What will you do now? I mean now you know that the accident wasn't your fault and you've no need to feel guilty?'

With no time to fully take in what she'd been told, still feeling dazed, knocked off balance, Sera said slowly, 'I don't really know. You see, in a way, I still feel responsible. If I'd said nothing about ending the engagement until we got to Pine Cove, the accident would never have happened.'

Keir's black brows drew together in a frown. 'So on the premise that we each have to be responsible for our own actions, what about Rothwell? *You* didn't drive that car into a tree—'

'Keir's absolutely right,' Cheryl broke in. 'It wouldn't

have happened if Martin had had a little more self-control. Still, that's Martin all over. As children we were both highly-strung and emotional, but I learnt how to keep my feelings under control whereas he never did.

'It's a good thing Kathleen knows exactly how to deal with him... Of course she loves him, which helps considerably, and I could almost swear he's getting fond of her. Last night he was as jealous as hell every time she as much as *looked* at another man.

'If you weren't there to...shall we say...*complicate* matters, I believe there's a good chance that things might work out.'

Then to Keir she said, 'What do you think?'

As though weighing up his words, he answered slowly, 'I agree with you that Kathleen loves him. While she felt sorry for Sera, the help she gave me was by no means disinterested.

'As to the other, obsessions don't last for ever, and it's not unknown for a man to marry his nurse...'

Just as he finished speaking, Roberto crossed the lawn and came striding over to them. 'Have I absented myself long enough?'

'Your timing is impeccable,' Keir assured him.

Roberto went across to his wife and, stooping, touched his lips gently to hers. 'Forgive me for being angry, *carissima*.'

They smiled at each other, their faces illuminated with the unmistakable look of love.

Her heart feeling as though it was being squeezed by a giant fist, Sera knew she would trade her soul if Keir would only look at her like that.

Turning to Sera, Roberto said, 'My dear, I hope you don't feel too bitter now you know the truth?'

'I don't feel at all bitter,' she assured him. And it was

true. The only thing she could feel at that moment was a
newborn, but growing, sense of relief.

Wanting to set Cheryl's mind completely at rest, she
added, 'If I'd been lucky enough to have had a brother, I
might have done the same.'

His smile warm, Roberto suggested, 'Shall we have
some tea?' Then to Keir he said, 'Or maybe you'd prefer
a beer?'

After an assessing glance at Sera, Keir answered, 'Neither, thanks. We ought to be getting along.' He got up and,
stretching out a lean, well-shaped hand, helped her to her
feet.

Cheryl rose too and, without hesitation, the women
hugged each other.

When Roberto had lifted Sera's hand to his lips and
clapped Keir on the shoulder, they all turned to walk to
the car together.

As though realizing that Sera's knees felt like warm
jelly, Keir cupped a hand beneath her elbow. Even so, she
was pleased to reach the car and sink into the front passenger seat.

A moment later they were moving down the drive, while
Cheryl and Roberto, standing arm in arm, waved them off.

'Where to?' Keir queried evenly as they reached the
main road.

Then, as though striving to be impartial, to make the
final decision hers and hers alone, he asked, 'Before you
talk to Rothwell, would you like to go somewhere quiet
for an hour or so to think things through?'

But her mind made up, she said without hesitation, 'No,
I don't need any more time to think. I'd like to go straight
back to Pine Cove.'

She saw his lean fingers tighten on the wheel, but rather
to her surprise he didn't ask her what she'd decided to do

when she got there. All he said was, 'Very well. If you're sure.'

'I'm sure.'

She needed to face things, to get it over, though the thought of what lay ahead made her nerves jangle and her stomach churn sickeningly.

By the time they reached Pine Cove, some fifteen minutes later, she felt even worse, if that were possible.

Without a word, Keir drove through the main entrance and parked in front of the house, making it plain that he had no intention of trying to hide his presence.

There was no one about and Sera felt sure that, on such a lovely day, everyone would be gathered around the pool.

If Martin was there too, it could be extremely awkward. She guessed that by this time, in spite of all Kathleen's efforts, he would have worked himself up into a fine old rage. And she knew only too well that, if he was really furious, he wouldn't hesitate to lash out at her verbally, no matter who was present...

Looking at her pale, tense face, Keir suggested, 'Would you like *me* to talk to him?'

She shook her head. No matter how much she dreaded it, this was something she had to do herself.

Abruptly, as though the question had been forced out of him, Keir asked, 'What do you intend to do?'

His intervention, his determination to get at the truth, had succeeded in 'opening the cage door'. Now it seemed he was satisfied to leave it to her whether she left the cage or remained inside.

As soon as the thought was formed she felt certain it wasn't so. Somehow she knew he wouldn't rest until she had walked free. But whether it was for *her* sake or his own, she was no longer sure.

Whichever, she could only be grateful.

Realizing he was still waiting for her answer, she said steadily, 'I intend to give him back his ring.'

His voice urgent, Keir pressed, 'No matter what he says, you won't change your mind?'

'No, I won't change my mind.'

The build up of tension in his big frame relaxed and, just for an instant, she got a glimpse of how relieved he was, before his expression was schooled into an impassive mask.

Jumping out of the car, he came round to open her door and, with the calm assurance of a man who owned the place, took her elbow and escorted her through the open French windows into the living-room.

Saunders, the head manservant, appeared as if by magic, giving credence to Martin's boast that his staff were always on the ball.

'Ah, it's you, miss. The master has been asking for you rather urgently.'

'Do you happen to know where he is, Saunders?'

'I understand he's resting in his suite, miss.'

'Thank you.' Sera smiled her relief.

For everyone's sake she would far sooner speak to him there, where there was no chance of any of the guests overhearing.

For a moment, knowing that Keir's presence would only infuriate Martin, she played with the idea of telling him she wanted to go in alone.

But there was a sense of purpose about him that warned her she would be wasting her time. Having got this far he intended to see things through.

With him by her side, she led the way to Martin's suite and knocked on the door.

After a few seconds it was opened by Kathleen who

cried softly, 'You're back! The good Lord be praised! Himself is out on the terrace.'

She sounded like her usual self, but her violet eyes held a look of uncertainty which changed to relief when she saw Keir.

'How are things?' he asked.

'Haven't I been doing my best to calm him since lunchtime? But without too much success, I'm afraid. He's worked Himself up into a right paddy.'

'Who the devil is it?' Martin called. His voice sounded harsh and irritable. 'I don't want to see anyone.'

'He wouldn't be expecting you to knock,' Kathleen pointed out quietly as she stood aside to let them both into the study.

While Keir paused to have a quick word in Kathleen's ear, Sera squared her shoulders and headed for the terrace.

CHAPTER TEN

AS SHE reached the French windows, Martin swivelled his chair. The instant he saw her, his fair face flushed with a combination of relief and anger.

'Where the devil have you been?' he demanded as she approached. 'I've been worried to death all day.'

'I'd take that with a pinch of salt if I were you,' Kathleen advised cheerfully as she came out to join them. 'Himself didn't get up until lunch-time.'

Giving her an impatient look, Martin turned on Sera. 'You haven't answered me... Where have you been?'

'Sera's been with me,' Keir stated calmly.

Looking up, startled, Martin exploded, 'What the hell are *you* doing back here? Didn't I make it clear you're not welcome? Why don't you stop hanging around Sera?'

Lounging in the doorway, Keir lifted a dark brow. 'If you tell me which question you'd like answering first, I'll try to oblige.'

'Don't bother answering any of them. Just get out!'

'It's only fair to warn you that when I go, Sera goes with me.'

Martin's smile held a kind of triumphant certainty. 'Sera won't leave me.'

'Don't bet on it.'

'Surely you got the message last night?' Martin taunted. 'She may be a deceitful little cow who's willing to sneak off behind my back but, when it comes to the crunch, she'll stay with me.'

He held out a peremptory hand to Sera. 'Come here.'

'I think you'll find she's through with taking orders,' Keir said quietly.

'Will you mind your own damn business?' Martin snarled. 'Sera...?'

'I'm sorry, Martin...' her voice was gentle '...but Keir's right.'

She watched him take the blow and ride it.

'Very well,' he agreed quickly. 'No more orders. But you won't leave me. We're going to be married.'

'I'm sorry,' she said again. 'I can't marry you. I should never have agreed to in the first place...'

As his face turned even redder, she hurried on, 'I'm fond of you, but I don't love you. I *wanted* to love you. I *tried* to love you... But love doesn't work like that.'

'There's no one else, is there...?'

Martin darted a malevolent look to where Keir had been standing in the background, but both he and Kathleen had gone back into the study.

'You're not going to tell me you love Sutherlands?' It was almost a plea.

For a moment she wondered whether to tell him the truth, then decided against it. To admit that she loved his rival wouldn't help. It would only add insult to injury.

Choosing her words with care, she said, 'No, I'm not.'

'Then, even if you don't love me, we can still make a go of it. You did say you were fond of me.'

'Fondness isn't enough. It just wouldn't work. You think you want me now but, in the long run, neither of us would be happy.'

'How can you leave me now I'm crippled!'

'You won't be crippled.'

'A fat lot you care if I am. Only last night you *promised* you wouldn't leave me.'

'That was when I still thought *I* was responsible for the accident...'

All the colour drained from his face, leaving it a pasty grey.

'I suppose in a way I'm still partly responsible,' she went on determinedly. 'If I hadn't given you back your ring, you wouldn't have driven off in such a fury...'

She found herself quoting Keir's words. 'We each have to be responsible for our own actions...'

'So you know,' he said thickly. '*How* do you know?'

'I remembered,' Sera lied hardily. 'I'm sorry, truly sorry, for all the pain I've caused you. I never meant to hurt you.'

'But I love you.'

'I don't believe you love me. I'm sure that what you feel for me is only an obsession... And no one can be responsible for someone else's obsession...' Once again she was unconsciously quoting.

With a feeling of release, she slid the ring from her finger and handed it to him.

This time he took it and, as he sat staring down at the glittering thing, she added gently, 'Love lasts, but obsessions don't... You'll soon be free of me and then I hope you'll be able to look for real happiness.'

He made one last desperate attempt. 'If you leave me you won't have a thing. No money, no job, no place to live...'

'But I can get a job and find somewhere to live and I'll have my freedom. In the end that's what matters most.

'Goodbye, Martin. I hope you can forgive me for not loving you.'

Head down, he didn't answer.

Though she knew she was doing the right thing, the *only* thing, she still felt like an executioner.

Turning blindly away, she stumbled through the French windows and into the study which, after the brightness of the terrace, seemed cool and dim.

Seeing her chalk-white face, Keir stepped forward and put a supportive arm round her waist. 'Ready to go?'

Taking a deep breath, she said steadily, 'Yes, I'm ready.'

'What about your things?' Kathleen asked with her usual practicality.

Keir made the decision. 'Can you arrange to have them packed up and sent to the Penthouse?'

'Of course.'

Sera gave the other woman a quick, impulsive hug. 'Thank you for everything. You'll take care of Martin, won't you?'

'Yes, I'll take care of him.' Kathleen promised.

Like a walking zombie, Sera allowed herself to be led outside and helped into the car. As she fumbled to fasten her seat belt, Keir slid in beside her and, reaching over, made certain it was secure.

A few minutes later they were leaving Pine Cove behind them and heading back to New York in the warm sunshine of a busy Sunday afternoon.

Leaning her head against the luxurious upholstery, Sera closed her eyes. It seemed an age since Thursday... Had it been only *Thursday* that Keir had erupted back into her life?

Since that unexpected meeting in the Park, so much had happened... He had lifted a burden of guilt almost too heavy to bear, changed her future, given her precious freedom...

But to do what?

Having just freed herself from one man's obsession, did

she really want to stay with another man who had admitted that he was merely obsessed with her?

Yet, even as she made the comparison, she knew it wasn't a fair one. There was an overwhelming difference. Martin had found ways to keep her against her will. Keir, she was absolutely certain, would never do that. If he knew she didn't want to stay with him, he would let her go.

But she did want to stay with him. She *loved* him. She *wanted* to be with him while ever he wanted her.

Though how long would that be? As Keir himself had pointed out, obsessions didn't last...

Astride the seesaw of uncertainty, she sighed deeply. Just now, she was too weary to think straight or make any decisions...

All the emotional upheaval of the last four days had taken its toll and, utterly spent, all she could do for the moment was be thankful for Keir's help, and lean on his strength...

When Sera stirred and opened her eyes, they were drawing into an underground car park. Recognizing it as belonging to the Warburton Building, and recalling little of the journey, she knew she must have dozed on and off for the best part of three hours.

Somehow, while she had slept, all her uncertainty had vanished. She had come to a decision and, serenely confident now, she knew she was going to grab whatever chance of happiness there was, however brief it might turn out to be.

Slanting her a glance, Keir asked, 'Feeling any better?'

'Much better.' She smiled at him.

Without returning her smile, he came round to open her door and help her out.

His parking bay was right by the elevator. He used his

special key and, in a matter of seconds, they were moving smoothly upwards.

Though she had been inside the Penthouse only once, and briefly, it seemed oddly familiar, even welcoming. She felt more at home there than she had ever done in Martin's apartment.

Or was that simply because Keir was there with her?

His voice coolly polite, he told her, 'There's a guest bedroom you can use for the time being.'

Remembering the ardent lover of the previous night, she had presumed he would expect her to share his bed.

She felt a sudden surge of disappointment, a regret that told her quite plainly that, subconsciously at least, she had been looking forward eagerly to the coming night.

Opening a door to the left, he carried the tote bag inside. 'I use the services here, so the bed's made up and everything's ready.'

He sounded as if he was trying to make civil conversation with a not particularly welcome guest.

'Do you want to stay home for dinner?' he added. 'Or would you prefer to eat out?'

Despite her long sleep, she still felt tired, unwilling to make the effort that going out would entail. But, wondering if *he* wanted to, she said cautiously, 'I don't really mind. I'll leave it to you.'

After studying her face, the lingering paleness, the faint shadows beneath her beautiful eyes, he said, 'There's plenty of food in the fridge. I'll throw something together while you freshen up.'

As she showered, she wondered about Keir's coolness. Last night he had been passionate and demanding, a man who had finally got what he wanted and had every intention of keeping it.

Since the morning, however, his manner towards her

had altered. Though he had stayed by her side and had taken care of her, that possessive warmth had vanished. He'd been detached, withdrawn, as though he was deliberately keeping his distance.

But knowing how scrupulous he could be when it came to relationships, she guessed that it was almost certainly to give her a breathing space. Time to think.

Well, she needed no more time. Her mind was made up. At the very first opportunity she would tell him how she felt.

Her mood a confident one, she put on fresh undies and changed into the skirt and the second of the silk blouses that Keir had provided. Then, having brushed out her tangled hair and twisted it into a smooth knot, she made her way to the kitchen.

Though it appeared to have every up-to-date convenience, with a range of comfortable-looking furniture and bright wallpaper it lacked the clinical feel of a lot of modern kitchens.

Several of the sliding glass panels which led to the terrace were standing open and the air coming in was warm and humid.

A tea towel knotted around his lean hips, Keir was tossing salad in a big glass bowl while, beneath the grill, a couple of steaks sizzled. The table had been set and a bottle of wine had been opened to breathe.

He'd also found time to shower and shave and change into stone-coloured trousers and a white shirt that, open at the neck, showed the tanned column of his throat. He looked up at her entrance but, again, he failed to return her smile.

Chilled by the coolness of her reception, the words she had been hoping to say died on her lips.

'I thought we'd eat inside,' he remarked. 'There seems to be a storm brewing.'

As though to add weight to his words, there was a flash of lightning and a distant rumble of thunder.

His manner that of a courteous but rather aloof host, he pulled out a chair for her and proceeded to pour the wine and serve the meal.

The steak was done to perfection, the salad deliciously crisp but, after the traumas of the past few days, Sera found herself with hardly any appetite.

Keir didn't seem to have much either, she noted thoughtfully. Though he kept his eyes studiously on his plate, he ate very little and without any evidence of enjoyment.

Sipping her wine, she made a pretence of eating while the silence coiled like barbed wire, pointed and painful, tearing her nerves to shreds.

She wondered what he was thinking as, his expression bleak as winter, he refilled her wine glass, leaving his own untouched.

He had fought hard to take her from Martin. Surely, having won the fight, he should look jubilant rather than like a man who was staring into the depths of hell?

When the meal was over and the coffee and brandy poured, seeming to make an effort to shrug off some of the malaise that was bothering him, he broke the silence to say, 'The storm appears to have moved away. Shall we take our coffee outside?'

Picking up her cup and glass, she led the way onto the terrace and took a seat in one of the loungers.

Keir followed and sat down beside her.

Their coffee cups were emptied and placed on the table without another word being spoken.

They had shared silences before, many times, but they

had been comfortable, companionable ones, not tense and strained like this.

Suddenly, determined to find out what devil was riding him, Sera asked. 'What made you suspect that Cheryl was hiding the truth about the accident?'

'I didn't exactly *suspect* anything,' he admitted after a moment. 'It was just a gut feeling that there might be more to it than met the eye. So I decided to try a spot of bluff.'

'I can't tell you how glad I am that it succeeded.'

'It wasn't difficult,' he said dismissively. 'Once I laid it on the line that I wanted the truth, I think Cheryl was actually relieved to get it off her chest.'

Her face full of feeling, Sera reached out a hand and touched his arm. 'But, if you hadn't gone over there and pressured her, she might *never* have told me. I would have married a man I didn't love and continued to feel guilty until my dying day.'

When he said nothing, she added quietly, 'I just want to thank you and tell you how truly grateful I am.'

Once again he failed to respond. There was something distinctly chilling about his hard profile, a studied aloofness, that made her withdraw her hand and relapse into silence.

Why did he seem so off-put, almost *angered* by her thanks? Was he just fed up with the whole thing? Waiting to wash his hands of her?

No, surely not.

But there had to be *something* to account for his attitude...

Perhaps, having achieved his aim, Keir didn't want her any longer? Maybe that one night of fiery passion had been enough to burn out his obsession?

No, she just didn't believe it. He had wanted her then

with a fierce, burning desire, and an inner certainty told her that he *still* wanted her.

Whatever was troubling him, it wasn't that.

So what was it?

There was only one way to find out.

Choosing her words with care, she said, 'I've been wondering why you put me in the guest room?'

Coldly, he asked, 'Where did you expect to be?'

'Sharing your room.'

His face set and hard, he remarked, 'It's obvious you don't have a very high opinion of me.'

Before she had time to tell him that was where she *wanted* to be and that his scruples were unnecessary, he went on, 'I heard you tell Rothwell that freedom was what mattered most.'

'Yes, but I—'

'So what are you intending to do, now you have your freedom?'

More than a shade nonplussed by the curt question, and unwilling to look as if she was expecting him to support her, she answered, 'I—I suppose the first thing will be to get a job. Then I'll need to find somewhere to live...'

Rallying, she added, 'Unless you want me to live with you?'

'I don't,' he said shortly.

'So will you come to see me?' she hazarded.

'No.' The monosyllable was uncompromising.

'B-but I thought you wanted me,' she stammered.

'You thought wrongly.'

Flushing, she cried, 'It's what you made me think! You said you wanted me back. You told me you wanted me in your bed—'

'Have you ever heard the old saying "Be careful what you wish for, it may be granted"?'

He watched as all the colour drained from her face leaving it paper-white. Then, looking straight ahead, his voice flat, devoid of emotion, he suggested, 'There's a position vacant at Sutherlands that might suit you. Christopher Redwood, one of my top executives, is in need of a good PA. The post carries an excellent salary and there's an apartment vacant in one of the blocks I own. It's unfurnished and it's on the poky side, but it would serve at least for the time being.

'Of course, you can stay here until you've had a chance to fix it up and buy some furniture... There shouldn't be much danger of running into Rothwell, even if he does come back straight away. Though I rather think Kathleen will have the wit to keep him where he is for the next few days at least.

'I'll see that you get an advance on your salary, so you'll be able to buy whatever you need without any financial pressure.'

Her heart like lead, Sera said stiffly, 'Thank you, but in the circumstances I don't think—'

'You've no need to worry,' Keir broke in sardonically. 'I won't be around. I'm planning to go back to England.'

'Planning to go back to England?' she echoed blankly. 'But I thought you'd come home to stay?'

'That was my original intention, but I've changed my mind.'

'Why?'

'Perhaps I find New York no longer suits me.'

She didn't believe a word of it. Keir had always loved New York. He regarded it as his home.

So why suddenly should he be going back to England? It didn't make sense. Unless...

Her mouth dry, she asked, 'When are you thinking of going back?'

'Tomorrow morning...'

Tomorrow morning! There wasn't much time. It might be now or never... And she would need to use shock tactics.

'I'll get a seat on Concorde,' he was going on, 'as soon as I've made arrangements about your job.'

She jumped to her feet, sending the brandy glass and its contents flying. 'You can keep your job and your apartment and your advance!

'Do you remember what you said only last Thursday? No? Well, *I* do! You said, "If you finish with Rothwell and come back to me, I've enough money to be able to buy you a diamond ring for every finger, and provide whatever kind of lifestyle you fancy—in short, give you everything your heart desires."'

Looking startled, he agreed, 'Very well, if that's what you want, I'll make you a generous allowance and—'

'You can keep your "generous allowance",' she spat at him. 'If you care so little for me, I wouldn't take a bad cent from you. I don't need your help. Go on, run away, why don't you?'

He got up, towering over her, his face furious. 'What makes you think I'm running away?'

'Aren't you?' she challenged fiercely.

With a short, sharp sigh, he said, 'All right, call it running away if you want to. But if we were both still in New York I couldn't trust myself to keep away from you.'

Her heart soared. So she'd been right all along. He *did* still want her. A year ago she'd been too proud to fight for him and she'd lost him. She had no intention of making the same mistake a second time.

Turning to face him, her green eyes holding a plea, she said, 'I don't *want* you to keep away from me. I *want* to be with you, to share your bed for as long as you want me.'

'Payment for services rendered?' His voice was harsh. 'You once told me money couldn't buy you. I don't want gratitude to be the currency.'

'But, it isn't...'

It was obvious that he didn't believe her.

She took a deep breath. 'In any case why should you worry about *my* motivation when you've already made it plain that yours was the need for revenge?'

Heavily, he said, 'Any desire for revenge died when I discovered the truth. You have a highly developed sense of moral values but, to a lesser degree, so have I. I find I can't ask you to exchange one cage for another.'

'But with you it wouldn't be a cage.'

'I fail to see the difference. You didn't love Rothwell and you don't love me—'

'But I do,' she said desperately.

'There's no point in lying to me. When I asked you, you admitted you didn't... And I couldn't help but over-hear your conversation with Rothwell. He asked you if you loved me, and you said no.'

'That isn't what was said,' she protested. 'His exact words were, "You're not going to tell me you love Sutherlands?" And mine were, "No, I'm not."'

'That's splitting hairs and, in any case, it makes no dif-ference. You may be willing to stay with me and I know I can make you want me... But that isn't enough.

'You're the sort of woman who should marry a man you love, a man who wants children and is happy to share a lifetime's commitment. The best thing I can do for both our sakes is leave you alone...'

For both our sakes... That phrase brought on fresh

doubts. Was she mistaken in thinking he was setting her free for *her* sake. Did he really not care for her at all?

But like a beacon in the dark came the memory of his tenderness, the way he had called her 'my love'. Surely he must feel *something* for her?

She decided to stake everything on one last gamble.

'Then, I've got problems,' she informed him crisply. 'The man I love doesn't want to marry me... And most men who want children usually prefer them to be their own.'

Keir gave her a narrow-eyed, assessing look. 'You'd better explain that last remark.'

'You made love to me last night. More than once. I could well be pregnant.'

'What?' he demanded.

'I could well be pregnant,' she repeated clearly.

'You told me you were protected.'

'That was over a year ago. My hormone imbalance righted itself and, after the accident I didn't take any more pills.'

'Oh, my God!' He sounded stunned.

'Of course, if you still want to leave for England tomorrow, I'll quite understand. No man likes to feel trapped, and I'm sure I can deal with things if—'

Grasping her shoulders, he shook her little. 'If you mean what I think you mean—'

'No, I wasn't thinking of abortion. Lots of single mothers cope alone, manage somehow—'

'I'm sure that's true. But I don't want you to be one of them. If you are pregnant we'll get married straight away and—'

She pulled herself free. '*Married!* Do you imagine for one instant that I'd marry a man who has just told me he wants out?'

'Don't be a fool, Sera. You know quite well it was *you* I was thinking of.'

'I don't know anything of the kind and, if you think I'd be willing to wait and see if I'm pregnant before you marry me, you've got another think coming! I wouldn't tie any man who didn't care a fig for me and you made your feelings quite clear when you said, ''Be careful what you wish for, it may be granted.'''

Ignoring his attempt to interrupt, she rushed on, 'You accused me of not loving you, but you don't even *want* me any longer, let alone love me.'

'Of course I love you,' he said roughly.

It was what she'd been waiting to hear but, knowing she wasn't home and dry yet, she said haughtily, 'There's no need to lie to me, just because I might be having your baby.'

'I'm not lying to you.' He sighed. 'God knows, I've never stopped loving you. That was why, when it came to the crunch, I knew I couldn't let you—'

Putting a finger to his lips, she asked softly, 'Do you really love me? If you do, *show* me. I'm tried of words.'

Stepping closer, she put her arms around his neck and, her face hidden against his throat, pressed her slender body to his. 'Please, Keir, make love to me.'

For a moment he hesitated and she held her breath.

Then he swept her up into his arms, saying huskily, 'Can't be too careful with all that broken glass lying around.'

Carrying her through to his bedroom, he laid her down on the king-size bed and, with barely restrained eagerness, began to undo the buttons of her silk blouse.

Drawing it aside, he unfastened her bra and, burying his face against the soft swell of her breasts, muttered, 'Oh, my heart's darling, if you only knew how much I love you. This last year's been hell... Please say you'll marry me.'

Carefully, she questioned, 'Suppose I'm not pregnant?'

Drawing back a little, he urged, 'Marry me whether you are or not. You once said you loved me. If I'd had the slightest hope that you still love me, I would have asked you the moment you...'

The words died on his lips as suddenly, sharply, his eyes were focused on her breasts.

Reaching out with fingers that weren't quite steady, he lifted the chain that lay in the valley between them. The look on his face as he stared at the silver ring it held almost made her cry.

Hoarsely, he asked, 'How long have you been wearing this?'

'For over a year. Ever since the night you discovered it was missing from my finger. The only time I've taken it off was last night. I was afraid that if you saw it you'd realize I'd never stopped loving you.'

'I only wish I had seen it,' he said fervently. 'It would have saved a day of hell. Fighting with my conscience, trying to persuade myself that I could make you happy, that I wouldn't be just another Rothwell... You see, until last night, I'd tried to tell myself that you might still feel something for me and when you swore you didn't, I was shattered...

'Woman, if you only knew what you've put me through...'

'I'm sorry.' She touched his cheek with a tender hand and ran her fingertip down to the cleft in his strong chin. 'But I thought, then, that I'd have to go back to Martin... That was why I was forced to lie to you.'

'So what are you going to do to make it up to me?'

She gave him her lovely, luminous smile. 'I'll think of something.'

'First, let me put this back where it belongs.'

Taking the chain from around her neck, he removed the ring and slipped it onto her finger. 'That will have to do until I can buy you something better.'

'I don't want anything better.' Drawing his head down to her, she kissed him with a sweet and tender passion. 'All I've ever wanted is your love.'

'It's yours.' He returned her kiss with interest.

'Will you always love me?'

Something in her tone made him lift his head and look at her suspiciously. 'Is there any reason why I shouldn't?'

'Well... I'm afraid I've lied to you again... And, now you *know* I love you and everything's all right, I thought perhaps I'd better tell you the truth.'

'I think you better had,' he agreed drily.

'When I told you I might be pregnant... Well, it isn't likely.'

'Why isn't it likely?'

'Because I'm still taking the pill. Though the doctor *did* tell me that the slight hormone imbalance I suffer from should right itself when I *do* start having children...'

Then, a shade anxiously, she asked, 'You're not angry with me?'

'No, I'm not angry. I hope we'll have a family in the not too distant future, but I can wait. It will be nice to have you all to myself for a year or so.'

Raising a quizzical brow, he queried, 'Now, you're sure you've no more confessions to make?'

'Only one.'

'And what's that?'

Mischievously, she said, 'I know you told me you

weren't athletic enough to enjoy making love in a car…but I once dreamt you made love to me in the bath…'

'Really?'

'Then you dried me all over and carried me back to bed and…' Drawing his dark head down, she whispered the rest in his ear.

Shaken between passion and laughter, he said, 'I think I can manage that, especially with a bit of cooperation.'

She kissed his chin and assured him, 'You can have my fullest cooperation.'

Interestedly, he asked, 'Do you happen to have any more erotic fantasies?'

'Dozens,' she informed him cheerfully. 'Enough to last for at least the first few years of our marriage.' Impishly, she added, 'I'm not sure what we'll do after that.'

Laughing, he assured her, 'By that time, my dearest love, I should be experienced enough to be able to think of a few of my own.'

If you enjoyed what you just read,
then we've got an offer you can't resist!

Take 2 bestselling love stories FREE!

Plus get a FREE surprise gift!

Harlequin truly does make any time special. . . . This year we are celebrating weddings in style!

A Walk Down the Aisle

WEDDING CELEBRATION

To help us celebrate, we want you to tell us how wearing the Harlequin wedding gown will make your wedding day special. As the grand prize, Harlequin will offer one lucky bride the chance to **"Walk Down the Aisle"** in the Harlequin wedding gown!

There's more...

For her honeymoon, she and her groom will spend five nights at the **Hyatt Regency Maui.** As part of this five-night honeymoon at the hotel renowned for its romantic attractions, the couple will enjoy a candlelit dinner for two in Swan Court, a sunset sail on the hotel's catamaran, and duet spa treatments.

A HYATT RESORT AND SPA

Maui • Molokai • Lanai

To enter, please write, in, 250 words or less, how wearing the Harlequin wedding gown will make your wedding day special. The entry will be judged based on its emotionally compelling nature, its originality and creativity, and its sincerity. This contest is open to Canadian and U.S. residents only and to those who are 18 years of age and older. There is no purchase necessary to enter. Void where prohibited. See further contest rules attached. Please send your entry to:

Walk Down the Aisle Contest

In Canada	In U.S.A.
P.O. Box 637	P.O. Box 9076
Fort Erie, Ontario	3010 Walden Ave.
L2A 5X3	Buffalo, NY 14269-9076

You can also enter by visiting www.eHarlequin.com

Win the Harlequin wedding gown and the vacation of a lifetime!
The deadline for entries is October 1, 2001.

HARLEQUIN®
Makes any time special ®

PHWDACONT1

HARLEQUIN WALK DOWN THE AISLE TO MAUI CONTEST 1197
OFFICIAL RULES
NO PURCHASE NECESSARY TO ENTER

1. To enter, follow directions published in the offer to which you are responding. Contest begins April 2, 2001, and ends on October 1, 2001. Method of entry may vary. Mailed entries must be postmarked by October 1, 2001, and received by October 8, 2001.

2. Contest entry may be, at times, presented via the Internet, but will be restricted solely to residents of certain geographic areas that are disclosed on the Web site. To enter via the Internet, if permissible, access the Harlequin Web site (www.eHarlequin.com) and follow the directions displayed online. Online entries must be received by 11:59 p.m. E.S.T. on October 1, 2001.

   In lieu of submitting an entry online, enter by mail by hand-printing (or typing) on an 8½" x 11" plain piece of paper, your name, address (including zip code), Contest number/name and in 250 words or fewer, why winning a Harlequin wedding dress would make your wedding day special. Mail via first-class mail to: Harlequin Walk Down the Aisle Contest 1197, (in the U.S.) P.O. Box 9076, 3010 Walden Avenue, Buffalo, NY 14269-9076, (in Canada) P.O. Box 637, Fort Erie, Ontario L2A 5X3, Canada.
   Limit one entry per person, household address and e-mail address. Online and/or mailed entries received from persons residing in geographic areas in which Internet entry is not permissible will be disqualified.

3. Contests will be judged by a panel of members of the Harlequin editorial, marketing and public relations staff based on the following criteria:

   - Originality and Creativity—50%
   - Emotionally Compelling—25%
   - Sincerity—25%

   In the event of a tie, duplicate prizes will be awarded. Decisions of the judges are final.

4. All entries become the property of Torstar Corp. and will not be returned. No responsibility is assumed for lost, late, illegible, incomplete, inaccurate, nondelivered or misdirected mail or misdirected e-mail, for technical, hardware or software failures of any kind, lost or unavailable network connections, or failed, incomplete, garbled or delayed computer transmission or any human error which may occur in the receipt or processing of the entries in this Contest.

5. Contest open only to residents of the U.S. (except Puerto Rico) and Canada, who are 18 years of age or older, and is void wherever prohibited by law; all applicable laws and regulations apply. Any litigation within the Province of Quebec respecting the conduct or organization of a publicity contest may be submitted to the Régie des alcools, des courses et des jeux for a ruling. Any litigation respecting the awarding of a prize may be submitted to the Régie des alcools, des courses et des jeux only for the purpose of helping the parties reach a settlement. Employees and immediate family members of Torstar Corp. and D. L. Blair, Inc., their affiliates, subsidiaries and all other agencies, entities and persons connected with the use, marketing or conduct of this Contest are not eligible to enter. Taxes on prizes are the sole responsibility of winners. Acceptance of any prize offered constitutes permission to use winner's name, photograph or other likeness for the purposes of advertising, trade and promotion on behalf of Torstar Corp., its affiliates and subsidiaries without further compensation to the winner, unless prohibited by law.

6. Winners will be determined no later than November 15, 2001, and will be notified by mail. Winners will be required to sign and return an Affidavit of Eligibility form within 15 days after winner notification. Noncompliance within that time period may result in disqualification and an alternative winner may be selected. Winners of trip must execute a Release of Liability prior to ticket and must possess required travel documents (e.g. passport, photo ID) where applicable. Trip must be completed by November 2002. No substitution of prize permitted by winner. Torstar Corp. and D. L. Blair, Inc., their parents, affiliates, and subsidiaries are not responsible for errors in printing or electronic presentation of Contest, entries and/or game pieces. In the event of printing or other errors which may result in unintended prize values or duplication of prizes, all affected game pieces or entries shall be null and void. If for any reason the Internet portion of the Contest is not capable of running as planned, including infection by computer virus, bugs, tampering, unauthorized intervention, fraud, technical failures, or any other causes beyond the control of Torstar Corp. which corrupt or affect the administration, secrecy, fairness, integrity or proper conduct of the Contest, Torstar Corp. reserves the right, at its sole discretion, to disqualify any individual who tampers with the entry process and to cancel, terminate, modify or suspend the Contest or the Internet portion thereof. In the event of a dispute regarding an online entry, the entry will be deemed submitted by the authorized holder of the e-mail account submitted at the time of entry. Authorized account holder is defined as the natural person who is assigned to an e-mail address by an Internet access provider, online service provider or other organization that is responsible for arranging e-mail address for the domain associated with the submitted e-mail address. **Purchase or acceptance of a product offer does not improve your chances of winning.**

7. Prizes: (1) Grand Prize—A Harlequin wedding dress (approximate retail value: $3,500) and a 5-night/6-day honeymoon trip to Maui, HI, including round-trip air transportation provided by Maui Visitors Bureau from Los Angeles International Airport (winner is responsible for transportation to and from Los Angeles International Airport) and a Harlequin Romance Package, including hotel accomodations (double occupancy) at the Hyatt Regency Maui Resort and Spa, dinner for (2) two at Swan Court, a sunset sail on Kiele V and a spa treatment for the winner (approximate retail value: $4,000); (5) Five runner-up prizes of a $1000 gift certificate to selected retail outlets to be determined by Sponsor (retail value $1000 ea.). Prizes consist of only those items listed as part of the prize. Limit one prize per person. All prizes are valued in U.S. currency.

8. For a list of winners (available after December 17, 2001) send a self-addressed, stamped envelope to: Harlequin Walk Down Aisle Contest 1197 Winners, P.O. Box 4200 Blair, NE 68009-4200 or you may access the www.eHarlequin.com Web site through January 15, 2002.

Contest sponsored by Torstar Corp., P.O. Box 9042, Buffalo, NY 14269-9042, U.S.A.

PHWDACONT2